Long Lightning

NORMAN A. FOX

A DELL BOOK

Published by
Dell Publishing
a division of
Bantam Doubleday Dell Publishing Group, Inc.
666 Fifth Avenue
New York, New York 10103

ISBN: 0-440-21049-6

Printed in the United States of America

Published simultaneously in Canada

December 1991

10 9 8 7 6 5 4 3 2 1

RAD

For my friend
TOM FAUSSETT

1

AMBUSHED

Here in the rocks heat dwelled, and danger; and at this crucial hour of siege Brandon had both a sharpened awareness of the danger and a sense of unreality. The sun, tilting westward, still got in a steady hammering; and he supposed the heat had turned him light-headed. Crazy, the way he kept staring at his right hand. A hand to depend on, browned by many suns and made hard-knuckled by toil, a hand holding tight a Colt forty-five, queer tool for a telegraph construction chief. Told him a lot about himself, that hand. Maybe he hadn't given it readily in friendship; no woman had ever offered to hold it, and some men had come to fear its weight, but he had laid it gently on horses and used it long in loyalty's cause. He stared at his hand and felt prideful yet displeased; it had performed much work, but there was all the work yet to be done and no chance at the doing. That was what a man forfeited with his life, the unfinished things, the many needs that were his own and others'.

Thinking this, he grew angrier at the bullets that sang from below, the bullets that dug at sandstone and whined away, making a constant reminder that he was a boxed-up man with time running out on him. Those men who penned him here showed a persistence that gave him a grim knowledge of their intent.

He had climbed this far, and he could climb no farther. He had the rocks around him, sturdy shelter against the bullets of the besiegers; but he had a cliff at his back, and though it was only twenty feet high, it was sheer and unscalable and made a closed door to escape. He had cartridges in his belt and the forty-five in his hand; and as long as he could keep an eye on the men below, he'd make certain none spread out to get at him. No rifles down there, he judged. But when darkness came, those men would rush him, and there'd be nowhere to run. That was the size of it.

From where he crouched, his sweat itchy on him and his thighs aching, he could see the broad sweep of the brush- and boulder-dotted land below, with the mountains standing yonder, pale and distant and misty blue. Trees up there, and maybe water, and cool grass in which a man could stretch. He put his mind against such thinking; it didn't make the sun less hot. Closer, a precise line of telegraph poles marched out of the south. He looked at the line with affection; here on another range, it was a new job started. Come to reflect on it, all his adult life had been measured out by telegraph poles.

Damn the sun that brought him nearer to his death. And damn those men who did all their talking with bullets and so kept him puzzled as to why they sought his scalp! He was sick of this business.

He shook his head and turned clear-minded and rebellious. Looking again at the telegraph line, he thought how his own life was linked to others, just as the wire ran from pole to pole. Sam Whitcomb, half a continent away, stood imperiled by the bullets of the besiegers; old Sam would be counting heavily on Holt Brandon to put through one more telegraph line. Jake Fargo, up at the construction camp to the north, would keep waiting for a man who wouldn't return. Likely the crew would say good riddance to a hard taskmaster, but they'd miss Holt Brandon when the going was tough. Some part of the hopes of all these people would die here in the rocks.

He caught the taint of self-pity in these reflections and put his mind against this, too. Better to wring out of each passing minute whatever came in the way of opportunity. Better to keep his head low and his gun ready.

A flurry of movement caught his eye as one of the besiegers wormed closer. For a moment the man showed, high-rumped and ridiculous. Brandon forced himself alert. Over half a dozen down there among the lesser boulders that littered the approach to the slope. Let one show more than a quick glimpse of himself and there'd be a sorry one with a singed hide. Brandon let go a shot just to keep them mindful that he still had a stinger. Gun smoke drifted back and wreathed him; it was a stink in his nostrils and an itch in his eyes. Queer, this shooting at strangers, this making a fight because they'd barred your way and gave you no choice. He was feeling light-headed again.

He squinted at the Montana sun. Getting low—mighty low. He looked again for his horse, lifting himself a little and exposing his head. He had a fondness for that piebald mare. He remembered the pint of whisky he'd rolled up in his slicker behind the saddle by way of doing Jake Fargo, his straw boss, a favor. Mighty odd favor, maybe, but he'd meant well by Jake. Yonder, he could see the attackers' horses, withdrawn a greater distance than a man could reach with a rifle, if he had one and was mean enough to make war on horses. His own mount had bolted at the first beat of gunfire that had sent him sprawling to the ground in pretended agony.

That had been two or three hours ago. He'd been heading southward from the camp to Salish town, riding along wrestling with some problem of construction when he'd found himself ambushed; and he'd hit the ground like a man going down to his death. The ruse had gained him the chance to make a bullet-peppered run to these rocks. Now, twisting his back to ease his cramped muscles, he wished he'd stayed in the saddle. The fire was hotter than the frying-pan.

Damned if he'd given up hope, though. He'd never cottoned to that kind of thinking. At thirty-one he could look back to the Texas of Reconstruction and carpet-baggers, and he'd piled better than a decade and a half of frontier years on top of those troublesome times— years when he'd strung telegraph wire from the Pecos to the high ramparts of the Rockies. What a heap of wire he'd strung, he and Sam Whitcomb! Gave him a tight feeling in his throat, thinking about those years. Now he weighed his chances again and found them mighty slim. Then he heard his name called.

"Brandon! Hey, Brandon!"

Twilight soon, and then the night would be coming on fast. His eyes squinted, Brandon saw a serviceberry bush move, though there was no breeze to stir it; and that heavy, guarded voice said, "Want to parley, Brandon?"

"Who's talking?"

"Sherm Lucas."

Lucas— They'd told Brandon in Salish that Sherm Lucas was the outlaw king of this high country, and the man's name gave Brandon an inkling of why he'd been ambushed. He risked raising himself so he wouldn't have to shout so loud. "You've cornered poor pickings this time. I've got eight dollars, a sack of makings, and a jackknife with one busted blade. Is that worth the fuss?"

"Come down here, bucko, and we'll talk about it," Lucas invited.

Brandon called, "You're making a mistake, man. Maybe you figure I'm packing a payroll for my crew. But I was heading *south*, to Salish, when you tried bushwhacking me. This was just a little jaw-and-grumble trip to our divisional headquarters."

"Doesn't matter," Lucas retorted. "It's *you* we want." His voice rose. "And we'll get you, bucko. You can make it easy for us, or you can make it tough. And when we do get you, we'll remember which way it was."

A cocky voice, Lucas's, not heavy and guarded when excitement got hold of him. A sure-of-himself-come-hell-or-high-water voice. Brandon ached for a good look at the man. Young, Brandon decided, but not careless young. The kind who showed you no more than the corner of his hole card. Yet that peek had been enough. "It's *you* we want," Lucas had said.

Brandon's anger rose hotly. When you worked for Mountain Telegraph Company—construction chief, no less—time and again you found yourself bucking Consolidated Telegraph, till you got so you recognized the old, old pattern wherever it showed. Wires cut and crews dodging bullets and supply freighters having trouble on the trails. That's what he'd been up against in Colorado and on the salt flats of Utah and in the shadow of the Sangre de Cristos. Now there was a contract to put a line through to a spot on Montana's map called Warlock. Once again he had to fling the long lightning of the telegraph across the mountain miles in a race against time. And once again the shadow of Consolidated was upon him.

"Come and get me!" Brandon shouted. "But you'll tell your Consolidated bosses you earned your damn pay!"

"You're calling the tune," Lucas shouted back with a laugh. "We'll do the dancing, bucko!"

Raising his gun, Brandon fired at that serviceberry bush; but even as he fired, he knew that Lucas had already eased away. The laughter of Lucas hung in the air and mocked the gun; other guns spoke, and the rock chipped near Brandon's hand. Grit drove at his cheek; he winced from the sting. Bullets ricocheted, singing their thin, whining song. No strangers, these men below; only an old enemy wearing a new and unseen face. Brandon bobbed down and fumbled fresh loads into his gun, his fingers wooden with haste. But with the forty-five ready, he merely held it, his ears strained for any sound that might tell him they were starting a rush.

He waited like this for a long time, and then the twilight was here, gray in the rocks, the sky showing the coppery red of the afterglow.

Getting on his knees, Brandon peered over the sheltering rock. Again lead drove a splinter from the sandstone; below, gun flame made orange splashes in the dusk, but the firing wasn't heavy. Time was working for Lucas now—time, and the descending darkness. Trouble was, Lucas knew it.

Yes, very soon now Lucas and his men would be able to spread out safe as so many sand fleas, perhaps to maneuver themselves to the cliff top above him, making a noose of men and drawing it tight. But now Holt Brandon knew that this was no chance attack, no haphazard try at swapping a few bullets for the contents of a dead rider's pockets. Well, he would give them a fight before they got him. Champ McCoy and his Consolidated bunch would have *that* to chew on when the report came in! In such a mood, he heard the hiss of the rope from above and felt it coil about his shoulders.

His wild thought was that an outlaw had got to the cliff top; and he swung around, hoisting his gun for a shot at whatever showed. Fear was a cold fist in his belly, but reason steadied him. Too dark now to see much, but instinctively he knew there hadn't been time for the enemy to have gained the cliff top. He'd watched them too closely while the light had lasted. Now a whisper floated down to him. "Tie the rope under your arms." He almost dropped his gun in astonishment. That voice had belonged to a girl.

This, Brandon judged, was no time for questions. Once you'd jumped from the frying-pan to the fire, no other move was likely to put you in a hotter spot. He got the rope tied in place and felt it tugged gently at first, and then he was hoisted off his feet and was being raised. Twenty feet to the rim, he'd guessed. Soon he was clear of the clustering rocks; he was like a spider dangling on the end of a thread, an easy target for those at the foot of the slope if they suspected what was happening. His sweat prickled his skin.

He blessed the darkness, and, blessing it, heard a gun blast. Lead nicked the face of the cliff, and again he felt the sting of a rocky splinter against his cheek. Another gun spoke, and another; a wild shout went up from below. Anger was in it, and disappointment. Brandon flailed his feet against the cliff, trying to get a toehold, trying to help himself upward. Hard-pressed he'd been before, but not helpless like this and naked to the guns. Then he was to the rim, and hands were heaving him to safety.

"Easy, now," he heard the girl whisper.

He scrambled forward on his hands and knees until he sensed that he was far enough back from the cliff top to be out of gun range. He hauled the entangling rope off himself. He realized he was breathing hard.

The girl was beside him, and with her was a man. The man was black and over six feet tall, a giant Negro. He wore range garb, this black Samson; and the girl had on a divided riding-skirt and a checkered blouse. This much Brandon made out.

The girl tugged at his elbow, saying, "Come on." Excitement had a hold on her; he could feel her trembling, and he wanted to steady her, to offer her his strength. He put his hand out.

"Come on," she said again in a low whisper.

Back of the shelf of land at the cliff top, a hillside tilted at a gentle pitch. The three moved on up the slope, coming to the top of the hill and over the hump. Just beyond the crest, Brandon paused, still and attentive. The distant guns had ceased banging.

The girl said, "Over this way! The horses are waiting!"

The stars were beginning to show, and Brandon had his look at her. Her face, though tight with strain, was pretty; her movements were pert as a young colt's. Brandon judged that her hair, mostly crowded under a sombrero, was soot-black. About twenty, she was.

She pointed, and astonishment touched Brandon again, for he saw the silhouettes of three horses which stood tied to a forlorn bush on this bald hilltop, and one of them was his own. He was as sure of the piebald as a man could be in this uncertain light.

The girl smiled, showing a flash of white teeth. She'd got hold of herself and was now a pleased one. "We came upon your mount grazing up north. That's what first gave us the notion you were likely in trouble. Then we heard the gunfire, and it drew us to the hill. We had to wait for darkness before we could help." Her voice turned more intent. "Sherm Lucas's bunch, I suppose. A holdup try?"

He nodded, letting her surmise stand. He had a cold remembrance of how tight that trap had been below the rim. He wanted to thank her, but their need now was to get into saddles and take advantage of the time Sherm Lucas and his men would take to reach their horses and work their way up here.

They walked to the waiting mounts, and Brandon took a canteen from his own saddle and offered it to the pair. They shook their heads, and he let the water run down his throat. When they were up into saddles, the giant Negro led the way; they put a silent mile behind them, heading northward across a starlighted openness in which all things were strange to Brandon and he was glad for guidance.

Timber loomed up and enfolded them, and they drove deep into the trees, a stand of spruce. Then the black reined to a halt. Brandon and the girl did likewise. The moon was just showing; it filtered light through the trees and laid lacy marks on all of them.

The Negro, dismounting, got on his hands and knees and put his ear to the ground. He stood up again, moving with an easy grace for all his bigness.

The girl asked, "Riders close by, Domingo?"

"No, Miss Ellen," the black replied, his voice, soft and gentle as a woman's, as surprising as the rest of him. Brandon found his skin prickling; there was something so primitive about the Negro as to remind him of a huge, black panther. No cabin-and-canebrake darky, this one.

Brandon said, "I want you to know I'm mighty grateful to both of you."

The girl measured him with a long look and held silent. Then: "I wonder if you'd be willing to prove that, Mr. Brandon?"

He started. "You know my name?"

"And your work. You're putting a telegraph spur up to the revived boom camp of Warlock. So far you've followed a straight course north out of Salish. But your post-hole diggers have been veering toward the west this last day or so. Does that mean you've decided to string wire through the Valley of the Three Sisters?"

He shook his head, smiling. "Now how the devil could you know that?"

"I've watched your progress through field glasses. So has Domingo. Your change in route was obvious. Now I'm asking you not to enter the valley."

He ceased smiling. "I hope you've got a good reason," he said.

"My reason wouldn't be important to you. It is to me."

He turned silent, thinking he heard the faraway beat of hoofs, but he couldn't be sure. If the giant Negro heard, too, he gave no sign. He stood grave and still, watching Brandon. A night bird rustled its wings overhead and passed its shadow across them; some small creature rattled its claws in the needle carpet of these woods.

"I'm sorry," Brandon said. "My reasons wouldn't likely be important to you, either. But I've got to go through the Three Sisters."

"I saved your life tonight," she said. "I didn't want to remind you of that." Vagrant moonlight touched her lips; they were red and full and showed a temper held in tight check.

"You don't have to remind me," Brandon said. "But what I owe you is personal. Mountain Telegraph is another matter. That's my job. I hope you'll have a chance to collect your debt sometime. From me. You can't collect it from Mountain." He supposed this sounded brutal, and he was sorry. He lifted his hands and let them fall.

She said, "They told me in Salish you were a stubborn man. Now I know they were telling me the truth."

He shrugged. He had met this sort of thing before, this lack of understanding of how it was with a man and his job. He wanted to say more, to make it plain that he was truly grateful, but the words wouldn't come. He was moved by her, and no denying it. She was alluring in the shadows; she was a woman harking up a hunger he'd long buried in the harshness of work. He could see the gentle swell of her breasts against the checkered shirt and smell a faint perfume about her that stirred him. But the pull of her was more than fleshly; he knew her to be a brave one, used to this land and its violence, and he judged her to be mature beyond her years and therefore like himself. If she had fire, she also had wisdom and courage; and a man's needs were many.

"I'm sorry," he said again. He lifted the reins and touched the piebald lightly with the side of his boot. "So long."

The feeling came strong that she might set that giant Negro against him, just as a person might unleash a hound. He had his gun, but he owed a debt to the black, too; it must have been the strength of Domingo's arms that had hauled him to the rim. His fear flared briefly and died; his obligation was a stronger flame. He fumbled at his belt for a forty-five cartridge and raised it to his mouth. He put his teeth to the lead nose of the bullet and bit deep enough to leave a mark. Leaning forward, he handed the bullet to the girl.

"You ever want my help," he said, "send this to me."

She closed her fingers around the cartridge. "Provided my need doesn't interfere with Mountain Telegraph's," she said.

He nodded. "That's right."

Then he was moving away from them, and soon he'd found his way out of the trees and was alone in the magic of the moonlight. He looked up at the stars and got his bearings; Salish lay somewhere south, and he headed that way. He looked back once, but he saw only the black chaos of the timber; and he moved forward, wondering if he would meet her again.

Miss Ellen, the black had called her. It struck Brandon that he didn't even know her full name.

2

DISPUTED PASSAGE

He moved through the darkness like a hunted man, letting the stars guide him and heading always southward, the notion sharp in him that Sherm Lucas and his crew might be about. Hot, they'd be, and hungry for the kill. He rode with part of him standing constant guard and part of him free-minded, his thoughts shuttling backward and forward, touching on today and all the yesterdays and the job that lay ahead. He could now guess how tough that job was going to be. He'd had his fair sample that afternoon.

Terrain he could understand, and the vexatious problems of stringing wire and keeping the supplies coming up. The devious deviltry of Consolidated was familiar to him, also. He could think a jump ahead of Champ Mc-Coy—he'd always done so before—but there could be the one moment when McCoy thought faster. Today had almost brought such a moment; he could thank luck and darkness and a girl and a giant Negro that he was alive. He could still sweat at the thought of going up that cliff with the bullets pelting about him.

Well, a man drew his pay and he took his chances. You got brooding too much about the risks, and you got jumpy when you needn't be. Your food tasted sandy and tobacco smoke was sour in your mouth, and every morning was bleak. The hell with that! He pushed the harsh thoughts away.

Twice on the trail south he heard the rumors of men traveling, the earth drumming faintly to the hard beat of hoofs. And twice he came down from his horse and stood with his hand tight over the piebald's nostrils. He waited, wishing he had Domingo's sharp ears. Both times the riders skirted him widely, clattering onward;

the second bunch lifted a yell into the night. It held youth and good-fellowship and a pure joy of living. Cowboys, he decided, homeward bent after a night of roistering in Salish. Whatever trail Lucas had taken, it was not bringing him this way. But Brandon's caution held till he saw the lights of Salish.

He came into a town that had slept across a dozen years and been surprised at its own awakening. The trading center for a vast section of mountain and prairie, Salish had suddenly found itself prodded to life by a mining boom at Warlock in the hills above. Now a railroad was building into Salish; a telegraph spur began its march from the town; and all the men who were drawn by the lure of the riches beyond came first to Salish to be outfitted. To Brandon it made an old and familiar picture, with only the names on the false fronts changed. You strung the wire because some need called for the wire, and that need brought people and violence and a great noise to the towns.

Into the straggling huddle of log and frame buildings, he rode in late evening. High-sided freight wagons rumbled along the narrow street, the drivers sweating and swearing and popping whips, the oxen showing sleepy disregard. The saloons roared ceaselessly, and men crowded the boardwalks. Horse-and-rope men, some. Booted miners, too, and railroad construction workers, and all the drifters drawn by the boom. Probably some of Brandon's men, too. They'd argue that those who put in solid shifts at digging post holes or nailing on brackets had the right to cut the dust from their throats or buy themselves a bit of love-making. He'd have to tighten up on them one of these days.

Through all the street's chaos, Brandon moved unerringly, stepping down from his horse and tying her to the hitchrail before a hastily erected building whose lighted window proclaimed it to be the divisional office of

Mountain Telegraph Company, Inc. Shouldering into the single room, Brandon smelled the mingled tang of green lumber and fresh paint. Two bracketed lamps laid upon a long counter with a row of silent telegraph instruments. There was a pigeonhole desk before which a man sat.

"Evening," Brandon said. "You're spelling the night operator, I see. That's learning telegraphy the hard way."

The man, Kirk Halliday, arose as Brandon swung the door shut. A big man, Halliday, the kind who wore broadcloth cut by a tailor and never got a grease spot on his waistcoat. A stocky man with stout shoulders and a good chest. About forty, Brandon judged. Montana's sun had already given Halliday's ruddy face an even redder cast, but the stamp of Eastern stock exchanges was still upon him. He came the width of the room and put his hand across the counter to Brandon.

"What kept you?" Halliday asked.

"A little trouble," Brandon admitted and shaped himself a cigarette. He stood leaning against the counter, a big man relaxed. He was tall, with the whittled-down hips and flat belly of one much in the saddle. He had hair the color of saddle leather; his features were rocky, his gaze direct. "Sherm Lucas," he added. "He and his bunch holed me up for a while."

"Lucas—" Halliday whistled softly. "The outlaw? You mean he attacked you?"

Brandon got the cigarette lighted. "That was the general idea."

Halliday shook his head and took on the look of one accepting the incredible without trying to understand it. He was a man used to a more settled land with softer ways. A handsome man, though his face was getting a little too fleshy. An ambitious man, impatient with small obstacles. "How are you coming with the line, Brandon?"

"Slow," Brandon admitted and frowned. "But we're just started. Once supplies get moving in fast, we'll really string telegraph wire."

Halliday shook his head. "The deadline's the middle of July, isn't it? Tell me, are you going to complete on time?"

One of the telegraph instruments began clacking, its metallic tongue loud in this little office. Brandon instinctively spelled out the message to himself: C-A-M-P T-E-S-T-I-N-G C-A-M-P T-E-S-T-I-N-G B-R-E-A-K R-E-P-A-I-R-E-D.

Halliday turned to the machine, a Wheatstone automatic, and read the tape, then fumbled with a sending-instrument and made an awkward acknowledgment. Brandon leaned farther across the counter, propping himself upon one elbow. He nudged back his sombrero; and seeing Halliday turn again toward him, the question still in the man's eyes, some perverseness arose in Brandon. This was made of weariness and the stress of many hours. "And if we don't complete on time?" he asked. "Will that break your heart?"

Halliday showed a flush of color. "No, but it will put a hole in my bank roll. I think there was a sneer in your question, Brandon, and I resent it. I'm no sentimentalist, understand. But I do happen to be a minority stockholder in Mountain Telegraph. I'm concerned enough over my investment that I've come out here to watch affairs in an unofficial capacity. I'm even learning telegraphy."

Brandon said, "Stay with it, mister. I'll tend to the wire-stringing." He wondered at his own rising antagonism and was half ashamed of it, finding nothing in Halliday upon which he could peg such perverseness.

"Look," Halliday argued, "this Montana job is more

important than it appears. You know as well as I that Consolidated is going to get the option on all future work around here if we don't complete on the date specified. That will mean a lot of business in the long run. Montana is a coming place."

Brandon nodded. "Hell, I know that."

"The first telegraph wire came in only fifteen years ago," Halliday went on. "Before the Indian wars, the telegraph out here wasn't very reliable, and it didn't connect all the important points. Two years ago the Utah Northern laid the first railroad track into Montana. Now the Northern Pacific is stretching out to the Coast. Railroad fever is a highly contagious disease, Brandon. Another few years and there'll be a web of steel in the territory, and that means a web of telegraph lines. It's opportunity, Brandon—big opportunity. That's what I'm thinking about. And this petty little Warlock job is the jump-off to all that will follow."

Now Brandon realized what had brought his ire rising, for it struck him that he and Halliday were as opposite as cat and dog. A hint of this had touched him at his first meeting with Halliday some weeks before. He'd listened to Halliday talk then and wondered how a man could see no more in telegraph-building than the swapping of a handful of dollars for a fancy stock certificate with curlicues around the edge and a hope for profit tucked into the fine print. Yet the irony was that he and Halliday served the same cause in different ways. Remembering this, Brandon now said, "Maybe I was a mite rough on you. I grant the truth in what you say." He spurted smoke through his nostrils. "I'm no sentimentalist, either."

Halliday gave him a quick, searching look. "I hadn't taken you for one. Stock dividends for me; paychecks and promotions for you. Is that it?"

Brandon shook his head. There was more to say. But

some things you kept for your close friends, and Brandon had only one. And even Sam Whitcomb was sometimes as hard to reach as the stars. Yet Brandon did say now, "Texas had some rough years after the war. A lot of Texas boys took to the *brasada*—the brush—and became outlaws. Who's to say where I might have ended if Mountain Telegraph hadn't offered me a job? I'll string their wire on time."

"Meaning?"

"Meaning I've found a way to outfox Consolidated. After today's doings, I'll be all the more pleased to tangle their twine. You see, they hired Sherm Lucas to dump me out of my saddle."

Annoyance showed on Halliday's face. "That's ridiculous! I know the Consolidated people. They're sharp, shrewd rivals, but they're also men of integrity. They'd never stoop to hiring killers."

Brandon shrugged, again feeling the rise of temper. *So you know Consolidated?* he thought. *Like hell you do! You've dined with their fancy Eastern officials, but you've never come up against a man like Champ Mc-Coy.* But he only said, "I won't argue with you. You asked a question, and here's the answer. I'm going to shorten the miles and shave the days by stringing wire through the Valley of the Three Sisters."

"No!" Halliday said.

Brandon folded his arms upon the counter and leaned forward. "So far I've followed the route laid out by Mountain's surveyors. It's a good route, so plain a blind man could find the stakes; but I'm wondering if it wasn't surveyed from a hotel window. The map shows a better, shorter way. Through the Three Sisters. I've studied the map and I've done some scouting. I tell you, it can mean the difference between winning and losing."

Halliday's face looked as hard and inflexible as a new

rope. "You can't do it!" he said flatly. "Oh, I know I haven't the authority to stop you. That belongs to Sam Whitcomb. But think, man! I've studied the map, too. It's obvious that the Three Sisters is the shorter route. But I've checked, investigated. The hills that wall the Three Sisters are Sherm Lucas's hideout. Through the years he's fanned out from the valley, stopping a stage-coach now and then, raiding a ranch, rustling a few cattle. Did you know that?"

Brandon flipped his cigarette at a brass cuspidor beside the pigeonhole desk. "No," he said. "I didn't. But whatever route we take, we'll have Lucas bucking us."

"You've got your teeth set in the silly notion that Lucas works for Consolidated," Halliday said. "Can't you see the truth? Lucas is obviously planning to expand his operations and make a killing now that this section is booming. But he's smart enough to realize that wires strung through the hills will make a web to warn posses and trap him. That's why he'll fight the line tooth and nail. And he'll bedevil us a dozen times as much if we work into the valley."

Suddenly Brandon was tired of this. "Is that all, Halliday?"

"One more thing. There's some sort of eccentric who lives in that valley. He ran Mountain's surveyors out with rifle bullets pelting around their heels. That's why they made their survey by the longer route. I got that straight from the head office. You can check if you wish. But I'm telling you if you tackle the Three Sisters you'll be asking for trouble. From more sources than one."

Brandon backed from the counter and jerked his sombrero brim with an air of finality. He started for the door, but at the threshold he paused. "Jump on the wire, Halliday, and get Chicago headquarters," he said. "Tell them I've gone crazy and am set to ruin Mountain Telegraph. Tell them I'm a stubborn Rebel who's out to fight a one-man war. The practice you'll get at the key will do you good. But while you're at it, tell 'em I'm stringing wire through the Valley of the Three Sisters."

"You can do your own talking," Halliday said. "Sam Whitcomb's here."

"No? In Salish?"

"A few miles from here. He came to the end-of-track in his private car. I was to tell you that he wants to see you. His daughter's with him."

"His daughter!"

Halliday made an impatient gesture. "Don't tell me you've worked seventeen years for Sam Whitcomb without knowing he had a daughter!"

"Gail," Brandon said wonderingly. "Sure. But she was a child the last time I saw her. That was a long time ago. Let's see, she'd be all of twenty years old now."

"And a handful for any man to handle," Halliday said. "Including Sam Whitcomb. You see, I've known the family for years myself."

Brandon nodded. "I'm obliged for the message. I'll ride out. Tell Jake Fargo, if he wires from camp and wants to know what's keeping me. He's straw-bossing the crew."

He strode from the office and crossed the boardwalk to where he'd left his horse. The town seemed even livelier than when he'd ridden in; sound eddied along the street in steady waves, a mingling of piano music and the cry of a saloon barker and distant laughter. Brandon had to shoulder among men to make his short traverse to the hitchrail. He let them feel his elbows; he was still angry from talking with Halliday and pitting himself against Halliday. Damn a man who thought he had a monopoly on the interests of Mountain Telegraph!

Jerking at the tie rope, he swung into the saddle. But before he could back the piebald from the rack, a man came striding along the walk—a lean, black-garbed youngster who carried a doctor's case. This medico, spying Brandon, came to a stop.

"Hello," the fellow said. "How are things out at your camp?"

Brandon remembered him then. Doc King. Dr. Jonathan King. Face on him like a poet and hands like a piano player, but Brandon judged that Doc King could snip off a leg if need be and never bat an eye. He'd met the medico before, when he, Brandon, had first come to Salish to start stringing wire from the town. Now Brandon said on impulse, "I'm glad I ran into you. They say you're a good doctor."

"Best in Salish." A ferment of joyousness and youth ran high in King tonight. "The only one, for that matter."

"What keeps a good man here, Doc?"

King smiled. "There's some nice-smelling mountain air in the locality," he said. "Walk out to the fringe of town and get beyond the whisky stink and have yourself a sniff. Then you'll understand."

Brandon shook his head. "I think there's more reason than that."

"Yes, there is," King admitted and turned grave. "I like this country, Brandon. A real town's going to grow out of this boom, and I'd sort of like to grow up with it. Look, we've got a railroad coming and a telegraph line already here. There's work to be done, work for everybody, the kind of work that counts."

Hell, Brandon thought, *everybody's dealing in futures tonight.* As if the future were a marked ace you could peel off the deck, never missing. The difference was that such talk from Doc King didn't anger him.

"Work is what I want to talk to you about," Brandon said. "Mountain Telegraph would like to retain you. That means you'll be down on the payroll and expected to check in at the divisional office here once a day. If a doctor is needed out at camp, you'll hop a horse and come fast."

King smiled. "You expecting an epidemic?"

"Yeah," Brandon said. "Of gunshot wounds." He crooked a leg around the saddle horn and rested his arms on his knee. "Tell me something, Doc. You must know every inch of this range. What's this about a crazy man who lives in the Valley of the Three Sisters and shoots at anybody who comes calling?"

King was done with smiling; he showed an older face, and his eyes turned guarded. "I could tell you a great deal about him," he said. "But the person happens to be both my friend and my patient. What's your interest in the Three Sisters?"

"I'm going to string wire to Warlock by way of the valley. It's shorter."

King shook his head. "I don't suppose my asking you not to would budge you any."

"No," Brandon said. "It wouldn't. You're the third person tonight who's either asked me or told me to stay out of the Three Sisters. I've a hunch that each of you has a different reason for trying to head me off. I'd like to oblige you, Doc. But I've got a job to do. And I think you're the only one of the three who would understand that."

King was less friendly now. "I'll not waste my time arguing with a man whose jaw is as square as yours," he said. "I only hope you'll reconsider before you enter the valley."

He nodded and moved along the boardwalk and was soon lost in the slow-moving river of men. Brandon watched him go. Then, shrugging, Brandon dropped his foot to the stirrup.

You could run into a riddle every which way you turned, he reflected, but that didn't change the fact that

you'd made your choice. No use fretting about the
Three Sisters tonight. Next thing was to get out to end-
of-track and see Sam Whitcomb and his girl. A mighty
late hour to be calling, but Sam had owl blood in him.
Brandon jogged his horse and began picking his way
along the street. He rode between the two rows of false
fronts, finding a sinuous way through the traffic, until he
got abreast of one of the saloons and heard his name
called.

"Hey, Brandon! Hold up!"

He turned in his saddle and saw the big, square-faced
man who stood at the head of the steps beneath the
wooden overhang, his figure silhouetted by the lighted
doorway behind him. He knew that set of shoulders, did
Brandon, and that hearty voice; and he brought his
horse about slowly and jogged her slowly until he could
look into the eyes of Champ McCoy, construction chief
of Consolidated Telegraph.

Brandon thumbed back his sombrero and showed a
bleak grin. "Well, Champ," he asked, "what's chewing
at you?"

3

A MAN REMEMBERS

A fighting man, Champ McCoy. A bare-knuckled, kick-
'em-in-the-crotch and bite-'em-in-the-clinches fighting
man, with all of an avalanche's impact in his big frame.
A man with vigor and a slam-bang way to everything he
did or said; but for all that, he had a smile to charm the
angels, when he wanted to wear it. He stood there in
the garb of his trade—pantaloons tucked into boots, a
plaid shirt, a rumpled corduroy jumper, a sombrero so
dirty and ill-used that no respectable horse would have

eaten oats from it—he stood with his hands thrust deep in his pockets and his smile like a campfire.

He said, "Brandon, it's good to these eyes you are."

"Sure," Brandon said. "You're as happy to see me as you'd be to find a cactus in your pocket."

"Ah!" McCoy sighed deeply. "After Colorado and Wyoming and all those places, I'd thought you'd call it a grand night when you heard me shout. We're old friends, Brandon. Sure and we've worked different sides of the fence, but we're wire stringers, the pair of us. Good ones. The best in the business. Are you so hard a man that you deny the same warm spot in your heart for me that I've got for you?"

Brandon brought his horse closer, so close that her fetlocks struck against the bottom step leading to the saloon's porch. The piebald turned her head and regarded him mildly. Brandon saw now the saloon's sign above McCoy. The place was called The Hogshead. The boots of dancing men shook the planking, but above their drumbeat came the roulette dealer's cry, "Odd and black. Odd and black. Place your bets, you buckaroos."

Brandon had got close enough to smell the whisky on McCoy and see the red network of veins in his broad face. A need to laugh built in Brandon, but he kept this need from showing. He crooked a leg around the saddle horn and said, "Get at it, Champ. What's really chewing at you? What fetched you here?"

"Why, I've come to pick up the pieces," McCoy said, still smiling.

"You're a little early, then, mister. Quite a few weeks too early."

"I've got time to spare," McCoy said. "And I'll enjoy watching Mountain Telegraph bust itself up."

"You've been waiting for that show a mighty long time, Champ."

"Situations change, my friend," McCoy said. "And money is the sinews of war." He teetered on his toes and rocked forward. He showed the face of a brutal cherub. "The talk is going around that bad investments have put Sam Whitcomb's back to the wall. Haven't you heard? You'll fail on this job and Consolidated will take over the wire-stringing in Montana. A happy day, Brandon. You and me will be on the same side of the fence then."

"How do you figure?"

"Why, I'll be offering you a job," McCoy said. "As my own right-hand assistant. I could use a man like you, Brandon, and be glad to have you."

At first Brandon's stinging thought was that McCoy had given him the supreme insult, like a slap in the face or the hurled contents of a whisky glass. Yet he couldn't be sure. He had known Champ McCoy on all the far-flung ranges where Mountain Telegraph had battled Consolidated; he could remember the struggles of the yesterdays, and always, boiled down, they had been fights between himself and McCoy. Fights in which contracts for poles or the hiring of the best freighters or the rounding up of a crew were the weapons. He had pitted himself against McCoy, never thinking of him as anything but the enemy, for no man save Sam Whitcomb had been personal to Holt Brandon. Not for many years, anyway.

He looked at McCoy now and wondered if there was sincerity in that great hulk, and wondered, too, if somehow the man you fought became always, at the end, your friend, because fighting was a shared thing and so shaped one man to be like another.

Yet it couldn't be as simple as that, not with all that had gone before and all that was bound to come. Strong in Brandon across the years had been the notion that some day the struggle between himself and McCoy would cease to be a thing fought remotely, and that they would stand toe to toe slugging. It was written down on the calendar. It was a day held in waiting by inscrutable gods. It was a fight that had to be.

"A job," Brandon said slowly. "So you'll have a job for me."

"The same as you'd have for me, if it was the other way around," McCoy said. "Isn't it a fact? Come inside and we'll have a drink on it."

A man laughed then; and with the laugh, Holt Brandon got a full awareness of the man. People had drifted in and out of The Hogshead, but Brandon had paid them no real heed. This one had come from the saloon and ranged himself at McCoy's shoulder, looking dwarfed beside McCoy, for the fellow was slight of build. There was wire in him, and rawhide, Brandon judged, for all his slenderness. The face was handsome in a wild sort of way and dark enough to hint of Mexican or Indian blood in the family. The laugh had an edge to it like a knife blade.

The man said, "A drink, eh? Let *me* be the one to buy, Champ."

Brandon looked him over. "We've met before, I think," he said, but he wasn't sure. Not certain sure. A lot of faces paraded before you in a lifetime. Some man who'd worked for McCoy on another range?

The slight one said, "You look familiar, too." He'd quit laughing, but the echo of laughter was in his voice. He brought the makings from his pocket and began fashioning a cigarette. He was dressed more like a working cowboy than a telegraph man. His hands were nimble. He got the paper rolled into shape and sealed and lifted his eyes to Brandon. "Swap the makings for a light."

Brandon took a match from the band of his sombrero and extended it.

"Thanks, bucko," the slight one said and struck the match and cupped it close.

That one word *bucko* did it, stiffening Brandon. When you squat in a nest of rocks and shout at another and he shouts back, you hear a different voice from the one he uses in ordinary talking. But a man gets to throwing certain words into his talk, and they stick out whether his voice is high or low. Just one had turned the trick. Savagery thrusting at him, Brandon lifted his gun from leather and leaned forward, bringing the barrel down hard across the crown of Sherm Lucas's sombrero.

Lucas pulled back his head—that was some reflex working—and looked up at Brandon. He stared in a startled way, and then his eyes rolled till the whites showed, and his knees caved under him. He would have tumbled down the porch steps but for McCoy's catching him. McCoy eased Lucas down to the porch's planking. Lucas's sombrero fell off, and a thatch of black hair showed.

McCoy put his fingers in Lucas's hair and said in a harsh voice, "His scalp isn't broken, but he'll have a bump the size of a pine cone. Now what the hell made you do a thing like that?"

Brandon still held the gun. "He gave me a bad afternoon," Brandon said.

McCoy was on one knee on the porch. He kept his position, his eyes brittle with anger and his smile gone. He was a soberer man than he'd been a minute before. "They say I'm hard," he said. "But I never want to be as hard a man as you, Brandon. I laugh when I fight, and I fight for the fun of it."

Brandon said, "Then you'd better tell your men to do likewise. This one probably rode in to get his pay. When he comes awake, give him another five dollars. He's earned it."

He dumped his gun and dropped his foot to the stirrup and neck-reined the piebald around and headed along the street. He'd thought to snatch a bite to eat before quitting Salish, but this interlude had sickened him. He rode through all the raucousness; he got to the eastern end of town and continued eastward; he rode into a prairie night with the stars a remote glitter and the breeze soft to his cheek. The moon still showed, but it sailed high and distant, not looking as though it had much heart for its work. At last the anger burned out of Brandon; his hands became steady. He rode with no feeling save the tiredness that came from a long day that had not yet reached its end.

Out here somewhere a railroad spur was reaching across the openness toward Salish from whence it would push on to distant Warlock. The telegraph line was up, and Brandon had only to walk his horse beside the poles to be sure he headed in the right direction. This part of the line had been put up by the railroad; Mountain's contract called for a start from Salish northward. He gave the line half his attention and took his pride in the thought that he could have done a better job. He supposed that maybe he gave too much thought to work; he had lived for nothing else these last seventeen years. He wondered if a man might grow to be like a telegraph line, geared to a direct route and dealing with humanity with the aloofness of electricity. He remembered Champ McCoy's face after Sherm Lucas had gone down; he remembered McCoy's last bitter words. He shoved this thinking aside.

Soon he came upon the camp of the bridge-and-culvert gang, which worked ten to twenty miles ahead of the graders and tracklayers who pushed the railroad across the prairies. The construction shanty was night-wrapped, the gang asleep, but an old man kept vigil at a fire. He was a hunched shape folded down beside the tiny blaze. He wore the faded blouse of a Union soldier with the chevrons of a sergeant still sewed upon the sleeve. Even now, all these years after Appomattox, you came upon fragments of uniforms, both blue and gray.

Brandon rode into the rim of the firelight. "How far to end-of-track?" he asked.

"No more than seven miles," the old one said. In the wash of the flames his face looked pinched; and after a first quick appraisal of Brandon, he showed a petulant boredom. "Those graders work as though Ireland's fate depended on it. One of these days they'll catch up with us at an unspanned draw and have to lean on their shovels till we get a bridge finished. There'll be merry hell to pay."

"You keep this fire going all night?"

"We've got tools scattered around, and a lot of light-fingered drifters have come in with the boom, they tell us." He shivered and buried his hands in his sleeves Chinaman-fashion. "For June, it can get mighty damned cold in this country before morning. You wouldn't be packing some of the hair of tonight's dog?"

Brandon fumbled at the lashings that held his slicker behind his saddle and got them untied. From the slicker he unwrapped a pint of whisky. He thought of Jake Fargo, straw-bossing up at the telegraph camp, for he'd fetched this whisky from camp lest it fall in Jake's eager hands. The seal hadn't been broken. He pared open the bottle and held it out.

"Glory hallelujah!" the old one said. He took a deep pull at the bottle and extended it back to Brandon.

"Keep it," Brandon said. "Cut down on those swigs and time them right, and the bottle will last you till morning."

"Why, thankee," the man said. He looked at the bottle, then thrust it into his pocket. "It's this old coat did it, I'll bet you. Third Ohio. You wore one once, eh? You'd have been old enough for a drummer boy, I guess. What regiment?"

"Hell," Brandon said, "I'm from Texas."

"For a fact? Well, Rebel whisky's as good as any."

"Better than most," Brandon said and rode on.

Another hour and he came upon the scooped-up welt of the grade, with stacks of piled ties beside it and dumped steel glinting in the starlight. Construction shanties loomed up, gaunt and gray. Deep-sleeping men inside them, readying themselves for the toil of another day. Hard and hairy men with the smell of peat smoke still in their clothes. Soon he passed a siding where a boarding train lay, the brightness of the night touching the windows of these bunk cars where more men slept. Thus far the steel had reached, and somewhere along here would be Sam Whitcomb's private car, shunted out of the way and left standing.

The thought came to Brandon unbidden: *I wonder how much of that whisky the old-timer's got left.*

He'd had that oldster stuck crosswise in his mind ever since leaving him. He realized that now. It was the blue blouse that had done it; funny how much could stem from some little thing like Sherm Lucas's calling him bucko, or an old man's clinging to a coat that was nigh twenty years old.

Take that same coat and forget what the sun and the wind and the rain and the years had done to it, and in your mind's eye you could put it on another man. Stand that other man up as sentinel before a courthouse door with a musket in his grip, and you traveled the street on which the courthouse squatted. A raw street, a dusty street. A raw and dusty town haphazardly on the Nogal plain, where the longhorns roamed and the ranch houses were a hundred miles apart and Comanche was still a word to make you look over your shoulder, remembering how a dozen of them had pleasured themselves with your neighbor's missus before they'd got around to killing and scalping her.

Yet your real hate had not been for the Comanches. When you were Texas born, you took warring with the redskins as a natural part of the day's doings, like eating and sleeping. It was a newer enemy that got under your skin, because he had first defeated you and then moved into your house.

What was that major's name, that fellow who'd been in charge of all those apple-cheeked boys in blue? Couldn't quite reach to it across all the years. Couldn't even remember the man's arrogance with the old sharpness of anger. Maybe he'd been a well-meaning man who was a little slow in the think-box. But in those days of carpetbag law when Texas lived under the eye of occupation troops, that major had been all the damyanks in the world rolled into one.

He could see the cornfield now, behind the Elliot place. And he and Buck Elliot belly-flat in the cornfield plotting. He fourteen years old and Buck sixteen, both of them fancying themselves heap big men. What Booth had done to Abe Lincoln could be an inspiration to any Rebel and a lesson to all damyanks. Buck even had the gun. It had been his father's, old Judge Elliot's, but the judge was being held at the courthouse by that Yankee major who strode so stiffly around town.

Brandon had wanted to be the one to fire the gun. And not from a rooftop while the major was parading the street. Walk right up to him and give him a piece of a Rebel's mind and then show him how much fight was still left in Texas. See if the damyank knew how to handle the sidearm he carried. That was to have been the ticket. But the gun was Buck's, and Buck wanted that bit of glory for himself. Draw straws, Brandon had urged. Make it an even chance. Draw straws, damn it!

Buck's face looked like a horse had stepped on it when he got the short straw and passed over the gun.

"I'll get another," Buck swore. "You ain't going to be doing this alone!"

Brandon could hear that voice now, in the Montana night; and he came back across the years with a start, the memory so vivid that for an instant he stared blankly at the long line of cars on the siding. No raw and dusty Texas street, this. He was sweating, and that surprised him; funny what an old army blouse could do.

He saw a car that was lighted and judged it to be the one he sought. It made a bridge for him to this night and this place. He rode toward the car and stepped down from his saddle and let the reins drop to hold the piebald. He set his fist against the door leading into the vestibule of the car and banged hard.

"Sam!" he called. "Sam, you old son of a gun! Open up!"

4

RAIDERS AT RAILHEAD

Whitcomb's voice, made woolly and remote by the thickness of the door, came to him. "Who is it?" This was the caution of a man who had lived dangerous years and known the dark ways of the bushwhacker. This was habit.

"Holt, Sam. Holt Brandon."

The door opened, and Whitcomb made a tall, murky silhouette in the dimness of the vestibule. He had no face in the gloom, but his voice now came clear. "Come in, son. Don't stand there growing roots."

"Sure, Sam," Brandon said and climbed up the steps. He felt Whitcomb's hand find his and tighten on it; he felt Whitcomb's other hand squeeze his shoulder. Eagerness lay in Whitcomb's fingers, and a great gladness. He opened another door and urged Brandon toward it, and Brandon stepped into the quiet world of glittering chandeliers and mahogany and red plush that was the private car. Seemed to Brandon that he sank to his boot tops in the carpeting.

"Halliday got word to you, eh?" Whitcomb asked.

Brandon nodded and had his first good look at Whitcomb. Three months since he'd last seen the big boss, for Whitcomb stuck more and more to the Chicago office these days. Brandon said, "You're looking fit, Sam."

He was not sure this was strictly true. Sam Whitcomb had always reminded him of a longhorn, lean and rangy and quick to move. Even in black broadcloth, with a watch chain heavy enough to haul a wagon stretched across his waistcoat, he looked as if he belonged to the *llanos*. His face was more lined, though, than Brandon remembered it from their last meeting. Maybe this light made it so. But Sam must be getting on—sixty now, or sixty-five. Across the years he'd showed no more age than a mountain. He had the sharp nose of a Yankee, but his mouth was generous and his eyes were warm. He had hazed Holt Brandon's destiny through all the thickets for nearly twenty years. He had a grin for Brandon now.

"Some brandy?" Whitcomb asked.

Brandon thought of the bottle he'd given away. "A couple of fingers," he said and dropped unbidden into one of the plush chairs and thrust out his boots. Mighty unelegant boots for these surroundings. Whitcomb kept the liquor in fancy glass on a sideboard, and he poured it out generously and passed some to Brandon.

"Mud in your eye," Whitcomb said.

Brandon took the drink down fast and neat. On an

empty stomach, the liquor at once loosened him and mellowed him. He remembered that Whitcomb's daughter was supposed to be here. One end of the car was partitioned off; beyond the door, he supposed, were sleeping-quarters, and Gail was probably inside. Funny that he'd nearly forgotten that Sam had a daughter. He'd visited Whitcomb's Chicago home once, but that had been—let's see—ten years ago. Yes, in '72. The child had been a beanpole with braids then, and he hadn't got much more than a glimpse of her.

Whitcomb asked, "How's the job, Holt?"

"Moving along. We've climbed out of the flat country. By the way, Champ McCoy's in Salish blowing a big wind in the saloons."

Whitcomb showed annoyance. "Hard on our heels as always, eh?"

"To pick up the pieces, he says." Brandon grinned. "He tells it scary. Are we really flat busted and ready to be cut into the culls?"

Worry crowded into Whitcomb's face and etched the lines deeper. He did not speak at once; he turned and set his empty glass beside the decanter. He said then, "You might as well know it, Holt. We've got our backs to the wall."

This surprised Brandon; he had put McCoy's talk down as no more than that—just talk. He looked at Whitcomb sharply and saw that Whitcomb wasn't joshing. He swept a hand to take in the elegance of the car. "This doesn't look like a poor man's hangout, Sam."

Whitcomb smiled; it was a poker-table smile. "In the prairie country, they build false fronts to make the buildings look twice as high as they really are. Long ago I learned a trick from that. You show yourself heavy-pocketed, and the world thinks you've got all the money cornered and your credit is sound. In fact, people are eager to give you money if they think you don't need it. Truth is, we've been going on credit for a good many months."

Brandon shook his head. "That part of it was always your end of the business. But I thought I was watching Mountain grow bigger, job by job. Hell, Sam, when I went to work for the outfit, you couldn't have got yourself a private handcar!"

"I know," Whitcomb said. He began pacing. "I started Mountain Telegraph with a ten-dollar bill and a secondhand transit. That Texas job, the first season you were with me, was my first independent job. We made a little money when we fulfilled the contract, but we'd still be a two-bit outfit if we'd had to build up job by job. That system is too slow, considering how narrow the margin of profit can be. After each job, I set aside money for the operating costs of the next job, then invested the surplus. Good investments meant that we piled up money fast and were able to buy better equipment, pay higher wages, outbid our rivals time and again. Do you follow me?"

Brandon nodded.

"Lately I've played the market wrong, Holt. A lot of investments that were sound before the crash of '73 haven't been good since, and somewhere I got out of step. I won't tell you how much money has gone down a badger hole. That's my worry, not yours. But we're in a split stick, son. This Montana job could get us out, for it will mean a lot more jobs. All the world backs a winner. But the loser gets kicked hard."

Brandon shook his head again. To him, telegraph building meant the stringing of wire across rough country; and these deep and devious financial matters of which Whitcomb spoke were a little beyond his full understanding. You put your faith in a man like Whitcomb, and you went ahead on that faith. You remembered that Sam Whitcomb had worked under Edward

Creighton in '61, when Western Union had been strung into Salt Lake City, closing the gap from sea to sea. You remembered that Sam could spin tales of the days when Indians had attacked and burned down the telegraph poles, and the men at the outer stations had lain scalped and naked beneath the prairie sun. You remembered that here was a man to tie to.

Now Brandon opened and closed his fist. "We go through the Three Sisters," he said. "No choice left."

Whitcomb ceased his pacing and stared.

"A short cut," Brandon said. "Halliday's against it. We talked about it tonight."

"I remember the reports," Whitcomb said. "The surveyors had trouble. Are you sure you're making a wise move, Holt?"

"Anything is better than having Mountain Telegraph go belly up," Brandon said, and he recalled Champ McCoy's smile.

Then he saw Gail. The door from the sleeping-compartment had opened soundlessly, and she stood in the doorway. She had drawn a wrapper over her nightgown; her hair lay long and golden on her shoulders, and her eyes looked sleepy. He was not prepared for the woman she had become. She had turned full-bodied and sultry, and petulance lay on her lips. That was because of the shape of them, Brandon at once decided, for her voice was pleasing enough. She said, "I heard you talking."

Whitcomb said, "You remember Holt, don't you, Gail?"

She came forward and put out her hand to Brandon. He struggled to his feet and took her hand and found it firm and friendly. He liked the way she shook hands; it was Sam Whitcomb's way. But her eyes laughed at him.

"Oh, yes," she said. "Dad's Texas wild man. The construction chief whose workers jump whenever he shouts. I have heard a great deal about you, Mr. Brandon. You seem always to supply chapter and verse when my father wishes to preach me a sermon about my shortcomings. I admit they are many. But I'd prefer to be compared to someone a little less rugged."

"*Abigail!*" Whitcomb said.

In Brandon there was both a growing antagonism and an acute embarrassment; he had the feeling of a man being flayed for no good reason. He was too tired for her kind of talk. He said, trying to strike back, "I've heard Sam read the riot act to a few. They always deserved it."

This directness startled Gail, and for a moment he glimpsed a depth to her that had not been at first apparent. Then her eyes laughed again, but for the moment she was laughing at herself. "*Touché!*" she said. "That's French, Mr. Brandon."

"We don't use it on the job."

"Do you do a good job?"

"The best I can."

"Then perhaps you'll do one for me. I've grown tired of bumping over this rickety roadbed and seeing a dozen shanty towns that all look the same. I'd hoped there'd be excitement on this trip. I'll count on you to provide it."

Brandon said, "This will surprise you. We lead a dull life and a hard one. You'll find that out at the construction camp, if you care to come and see for yourself. Just keep from underfoot while you're there."

She looked at her father. "Is he always this insolent?" she asked with amusement.

Whitcomb said very quietly, "Go back to bed, Gail. We've got business to discuss."

"Of course," she said and turned meekly and headed for the sleeping quarters. At the door she looked back and smiled, thus showing her meekness to have been a pose. Hers was a mischievous smile, and some of the rancor went out of Brandon. He guessed that she was a child turned woman in body only, yet he wasn't sure. He remembered Miss Ellen, otherwise nameless, who had shown a mature courage and a mature intent.

"Good night, Mr. Brandon," Gail said and winked at him as she closed the door behind her.

Sam Whitcomb spread his hands and said wearily, "I apologize for her, Holt."

Brandon said, "I hope she stays clear of the construction camp. This is no tea party we're going to be staging."

Whitcomb shook his head. "I've licked everything in my life but her. She was an autumn child, Holt, and motherless after her tenth year. I broke her to ride side-saddle, when all the while I really wanted her to be Injun. She's a spoiled brat, and I'm not fooled about that. I'd have left her at home if I'd had spine enough to buck her. All I ask is that you remember that she's never known the kind of life we've known." He looked worried. "No, it's not that simple. I've got to ask even more."

Brandon said, "That I keep her from finding it dull out here?"

"No," Whitcomb said. "That you keep her from kicking over the traces. There's a man."

"Yes," Brandon said thoughtfully. "There would be."

"Kirk Halliday, as a matter of fact."

This truly surprised Brandon. "Him? He could damn near be her father!"

"Maybe that's part of what attracts her. They were engaged a year. Kirk thought that having a hackamore on her meant she was as good as bridled. That's where he made his mistake. But she knows he's out here, and I think that was half the reason she chose to come along. She's willful, Holt. That's my fault, too; I couldn't be a proper father to her, not and be all over the frontier in the years when she was growing up. But there's a lot of good in the girl. Help me keep a hold on her."

Brandon made another fist out of his hand and stared at it. Having to save Mountain Telegraph wasn't enough, he was thinking; now he was supposed to save Whitcomb's daughter from her own foolishness, too. He looked up at Whitcomb and wondered how genuine was his affection for this man and how much of his feeling was actually the habit of servitude and long association. It was a thing not clear to him. It had never been.

He said, trying to pick up the broken thread of their talk, "About that route through the Valley of the Three Sisters—"

Whitcomb nodded. "I'll trust your judgment on that, Holt. Yet I can't forget the surveyors' reports." He paced for several minutes, thinking deeply, a man beset from all sides. He looked up. "Your glass is empty, Holt. More brandy?"

Brandon shook his head. "Not tonight."

Then Brandon came to his feet, startled. A boot had kicked hard at the door leading in from the vestibule, and his single thought was that Whitcomb must have forgotten to lock the outer door after admitting him.

Two men lurched into the car, one crowding behind the other. Two bandanna-masked men with slickers drawn over their outer clothes further to conceal their identities. Guns were in their hands, and that was what kept Brandon from trying for his own weapon—that and the certainty of whom he was pitted against. Nothing could hide that set of shoulders or the blocky bigness of the man in the lead, and Brandon knew that second, slighter figure, too. His next thought was that he hadn't put Sherm Lucas to sleep for long.

He said, "What the hell is this, Champ?"

McCoy's voice came muffled through the bandanna.

"Sure, and you'll find out. Just get your hands up and put your face to the wall, Brandon. You too, Whitcomb."

Whitcomb, his eyes unbelieving, looked at Brandon and asked, "Champ McCoy?"

"Gone crazy!" Brandon said.

"Like a fox." McCoy chuckled deep in his throat. He moved his gun back and forth so the barrel covered the width of the car. "Do as you're told!"

What was it Kirk Halliday had said? "I know the Consolidated people— They'd never stoop to hiring killers." *Hell,* Brandon thought, *he ought to be dancing at this fandango!*

It was Lucas who worried him most—Lucas, who'd got a cracked skull and would be itching to pay back for it. McCoy couldn't be discounted, either, not when McCoy got bold enough for a play like this. Danger had crowded into the car, and no mistake about it; and in the hush on the heels of McCoy's words, the smashing of glass filled the car with sound.

One of the windows had blossomed a jagged star; and Brandon's wild notion was that Sherm Lucas had let go with a random, intimidating shot. But common sense blew a cool breath on his thinking, and he knew at once that this wild pair would not want any unnecessary fireworks that would rouse the boarding train and bring the workers spilling from their bunks.

And then he understood.

Another star blossomed on the glass. This time Brandon heard a rifle bark far out in the night. Someone in the yonder darkness had seen the two masked ones through the lighted window and was taking a hand in this.

Brandon leaped sideways and fell into a crouch. McCoy had turned and was bolting, almost bowling over Lucas in his haste. At once the two of them were in the vestibule and, from the sound they made, crowding through the outer door. Brandon got his gun out. He saw Whitcomb's strained, still-puzzled face; he got a glimpse of the door to the sleeping-compartment. It was open again, and Gail stood there, her eyes startled.

Brandon moved then, charging toward the vestibule. He got into it and found the outer door open and leaped to the slope of the grade. He landed hard and fought for balance. He stood peering; along the row of cars two hunched figures ran. Distantly, Brandon made out the silhouettes of horses.

He let go with a shot and knew as he fired that he'd missed. He saw McCoy and Lucas swing up into saddles and lift their horses to a gallop. He ran to his own waiting piebald and caught up the reins. The boarding train was aroar with excitement, and the first of the workmen were already spilling out. They got between Brandon and the two fleeing horsemen, and he did not fire again. He looked out across the starlit prairie whence those rifle shots had come. No moon now, but he saw another horseman dimly. This one bulked immense in his saddle and lifted a rifle in a flourish as he rode off.

"Domingo!" Brandon called. "Domingo, come back here!" But the giant black paid no heed, and the thought ran in Brandon: *Twice in his debt now!* And he knew that Domingo must have been shadowing him ever since he'd quit the man in the timber above Salish.

He pulled himself to the back of his mount. Whitcomb was on the steps of his private car; his voice lifted above the excited shouts of the half-dressed workmen who swarmed along the grade. "Wait, Holt!" Whitcomb cried. "Where you going?"

"To the camp," Brandon shouted. "Better post a guard the rest of the night. I don't think our friends will be back, though. They've got a bellyful. But they've showed how bold Consolidated has turned."

"Sleep here tonight," Whitcomb urged.

Brandon shook his head. "I want to be nearer the camp when the sun comes up. There's wire to be strung, and it's time to get at it." He neck-reined his horse around. "I'm taking that shortcut I told you about, Sam. Tonight clinches it. I'll see you later."

5

THE CRAZY ONE

He got no farther than Salish on his return ride, and there tiredness became a club that drove him from his saddle. He hit town in a small, hushed hour that lay between midnight and morning and found the street swept clean of raucousness as though a great wind had blown the blatancy out of Salish. Windows were dead eyes staring at him. By fading starlight a lone, drunken wayfarer lurched along, a gaunt dog at his heels; and when Brandon stepped down from saddle, his own boots beat out hollow echoes that pursued him along the boardwalk.

He put the piebald in the wagon yard behind Mountain's divisional office where wagons and piled supplies stood gauntly outlined; and he walked wearily to the Ballard house, the hotel where Halliday stayed. A drowsy desk clerk took his signature and gave him a key, and he climbed to the room indicated and let himself in.

Only the town had a different name, and the hotel, he reflected. He had seen this faded carpeting by this same smoky lamplight in a score of frontier places; even the wallpaper seemed familiar, and the chipped basin and bowl. The calendar on the wall was two years old and advertised a St. Louis merchandising house that dealt in mining machinery. The bed had a swaybacked look, and he hoped it was not too rampageous with livestock. He wondered if bedbugs were a migratory breed that followed a telegraph man from one town to another. Smiling at the thought, he got out of his boots and hung his gun belt over a post of the bed, blew out the lamp, and crawled under the blankets.

He'd locked the door, but he supposed he should have propped a chair under the knob as well, for he was remembering Champ McCoy and Sherm Lucas and their boldness tonight. Too tired to get up and barricade the door, he thought: *The hell with them!* Yet sleep did not come at once. He had bedded under the stars so many nights, or within the canvas of a Mountain Telegraph tent, that walls seemed to push at him and the ceiling was like the lid of a coffin. He lay listening to the creak of this clapboard building; plainly to him came the protest of bedsprings as his next-door neighbor turned over. Someone snored lustily farther along the hall; and once he thought he heard the laughter of a woman, or perhaps the sobbing of one.

Last morning was something remembered from another life. The afternoon, too, with its siege and shooting, was distant as Dallas. He'd pitted himself against too many people, he guessed, and had been drained dry by the constant fight.

First there'd been Sherm Lucas and his crew, and then he'd put his will against Miss Ellen's. In Salish he'd tasted the antagonism of Kirk Halliday and touched a sore spot with Doc King when the eccentric of the Three Sisters had been mentioned. You'd think that crazy one was King's best friend! Then there'd been the saloon-porch meeting with Champ McCoy and Sherm Lucas, and afterward he'd ridden out and found an old man in a faded blue coat and given him a pint of whisky. That was a warm remembrance, yet it harked his mind back to the bitter thinking that had come from the sight of the coat. He now realized that on his return to Salish he had ridden wide of the bridge-and-culvert gang's camp, not knowing why. He had seen the eye of the old man's lonely fire across the night and so known that that nameless one still kept his vigil.

That girl, Gail. She arose in the darkness behind his closed eyelids and was a soft, full-bodied creature, so exciting that he put away the thought, finding in it some disloyalty to Sam Whitcomb. Damned if the girl hadn't rubbed his fur the wrong way with her spoiled-brat airs and her crosswise notion that Holt Brandon was supposed to make the West woolly for her! And Sam Whitcomb hadn't brought him any balm with the admission that Mountain Telegraph was indeed hard-pressed and shaky. But of all the day's doings, the coming of McCoy and Sherm Lucas, guns in hands, had been the corker.

He wondered now, as he'd wondered in the car and on the return ride to Salish, what had moved the pair to so desperate an act. Maybe Lucas, wild-mad after that clout on the cranium, had wanted revenge and had followed him, Brandon, to even up. But Champ McCoy would have backed no such loco notion. Champ could be a rough one in the clinches, but he played safe. A bullet from the bushes would be more to the pattern of all of McCoy's past deviltry. But tonight he'd been bolder. Whitcomb, then? Had they been going to kill old Sam and so leave Mountain Telegraph leaderless?

No answers rose out of the hotel room's darkness, and even thinking became like carrying a stone on top of his head, so Brandon turned over and willed himself to sleep. He awoke in the grayness of dawn, for that, also, was his will; and while Salish still slumbered, he dressed and came down to the street. An old gray tomcat in the morning light, this town. Brandon rattled the locked screen on a Chinese restaurant and so became the first customer of the day; and twenty minutes later, while the town still lay murky and silent, he rode out toward the north.

Ahead the hills showed high and fog-wrapped. He rode beside the telegraph line that he had built, and he thought of all the miles yet to be crossed by pine poles and wire; and time became like a giant's hand, pressing at him. He rode impatiently yet with a certain gladness; the questions of the night could answer themselves, and there was no use fretting about things that were beyond understanding. Work was something knowledgeable and waiting. His hands itched for the work, and he leaned forward and lifted the mare to a high gallop.

String wire, and you follow a routine in which each day is like the one before, except for the shifts of weather and the particular problems of that day. Even the problems form a repeated pattern of annoyance, so that when a wagon wheel breaks or the cook oversalts the stew or the camp tents blow down in a high wind, you get the feeling that things have happened before and will happen again. Trouble shows a dozen familiar faces and thus is no stranger come to roost. Days tramp upon the heels of days until you couldn't swear whether it was Sunday or Christmas or half past seven, and the only day distinguishable from another is the one marked down in your mind, the one when your job will stand completed or failure will grin at you.

So it was with Holt Brandon that week after Salish. Each day was full from dawn to dusk and even beyond the darkness, when huge brush fires lighted the scene for overtime workers. Kept a man humping just to boss all the crew. Kept a man's tongue busy, driving them.

With his crew divided into three sections, the vanguard bunch dug post holes, the men strung out along the line, each digging four feet deep into the stubborn ground. The last man of the string, finishing his job, walked to the front of the line, paced off the proper distance, and began digging again. Thus they made a revolving chain of humanity, pressing always forward.

The second group cut poles and set them; the third strung wire. There was even a man to follow up, trimming off any tree branches that touched the wire in this timbered, broken country that climbed toward the hills. Years of this sort of construction had taught Brandon how to wring teamwork from a crew, and his big job was to be sure some of his men did not shirk. He sweated with them and was everywhere at once.

Mountain Telegraph's equipment was good—sturdy wagons and rain-tight tents, a cooking-stove and all the utensils. And the crew ate well. The men were experienced; they'd strung wire on other ranges, all of them; and the problem, as always, was one of supply. But with Salish as their base, and their own newly strung wire to flash back word of their various needs, they tried to keep the freight wagons rumbling between railhead and this wilderness outpost.

Sam Whitcomb was in Salish now, holding forth at divisional headquarters by day and returning to his private car each night. Sam was one who could understand that when a construction chief bellowed for insulators, he wanted insulators. And Halliday was there, too, running errands for the big boss and otherwise making himself useful. But what of McCoy and Lucas, Brandon wondered.

No cut wires these days. No pelting rifle bullets; nothing but the constant and ordinary troubles that came with crossing such terrain.

Yet Brandon kept guards posted, though when you robbed a man of sleep you did not get his full effort the next day. There were no gay hours around a campfire, once the day's shift was done, no mock court by which the men jokingly tried each other for infractions of rules. It was bed down fast, boys, if you aren't working an overtime shift. Morning's coming soon.

This was Brandon's way of conducting a camp; it had always been his way when a race was on. He was a remote spirit, apart from his men; he was the constant spur, urging them on. He had their respect, but he owned little of their affection. This he read in their eyes when he gave them a bit of his tongue.

Some he knew from way back, for a few were veterans even older than he in the service of Sam Whitcomb. Jake Fargo, for instance, whiskery and given to fighting the bottle on pay days. He'd worked with Whitcomb on Western Union and could tell you how they'd scared respect for the white man's magic into those two Indian chiefs, Washakie and Winnemucca, by having them talk over the telegraph wire and then bringing them by Overland stage to a juncture point halfway across the five hundred miles that had separated them. A surprised pair of redskins they'd been, Jake reported, when they compared what they'd talked about and realized how fast the long lightning had carried their words. But later on, the Indians had got over their awe of the telegraph, you bet. They'd soon savvied that troop movements were ordered by telegraph, and they'd taught themselves a smart trick of cutting the wire, then splicing it with buckskin, so that a man could look forever for the break.

Well, there were no troublesome Indians in Montana to buck Mountain Telegraph. Not these days. And though the last of the buffalo seemed to have moved south from Saskatchewan into Montana, they were few compared to the mighty herds that had once blackened the prairies from skyline to skyline. No poles getting rubbed down by their shaggy backs in this hilly country. Western Union had once got the notion of placing sharp spikes in the poles to discourage the buffalo. But Western Union had given up that idea fast. The buffalo had loved those improvised combs.

Those had been the problems of another day; Brandon had his own, but always the work went on. Six men to nail the brackets on the poles and raise and set them. Four men and one team to string the wire and put it on the poles. The teamster had other work as well; he had to move camp and aid the cook. Each morning the wagon was loaded with the cooking-outfit and tents and driven to the place where the farthermost men would end their day's work. Each night the camp was pitched anew, until one night they were into the broadness of the Valley of the Three Sisters, the grassy, tree-dotted expanse spreading before them.

A good country, Brandon decided as he sat his saddle and looked upon it. A country where he could cut down the construction hours. Trees ready at hand to provide poles. He set his eyes on the three distant hills that gave the valley its name and remembered that Warlock lay high on the hill that stood farthest to the west. He measured the distance with his eye and counted the days that were left and got a tight feeling in his belly.

Kirk Halliday came riding up from Salish in an open buggy the next morning. He stayed on the seat and had his look around, his ruddy face alive with interest, and then drove up ahead to where Brandon was directing the operations of the post-hole diggers. Halliday raised a hand in salute and cleared his throat. "I've had a long talk with Sam Whitcomb, Brandon. He's approved your change of route. He said your judgment has never failed him yet. He knows your record better than I do. Maybe I was hasty the other night."

As green an olive branch as a man could offer him, Brandon admitted in his mind. What was the use of wondering how it would taste if you bit into it? "Supplies have been coming through steady," he said.

"That's Salish's doing. Likely you've had a hand in seeing that everything runs smooth down there. I'm grateful, mister. I'll be wiring my thanks from Warlock in a few weeks."

Halliday scanned the sweep of valley to the northward, his hand shielding his eyes. "Any trouble with the eccentric who ran our surveyors out of here?"

"The crazy one? Not a sign of him."

"Good." Halliday grunted and was soon on his way southward again, his buggy like a black beetle in the distance. Brandon, watching him go, shook his head. Halliday clung hard to his worry about the eccentric.

But the next day the camp had a second visitor, and a third.

The advance post-hole digger saw one first, and his yell fetched Brandon on the bound. Topping a slight rise to the west and so sky-lined was a tall, stately rider, lean of face, with a carefully trimmed silvery beard. This was the land of the man on horseback, but the queer note was the man's garb. For he wore the full regalia of a Confederate colonel of cavalry, complete to the saber; he wore it in the manner of one who habitually dressed thus. No tattered coat, this one.

The post-hole digger spat a stream of tobacco juice. "Now what the hell!" he said to nobody. "Is this Confederate Memorial Day?"

Brandon had a sense of being flung backward in time. "Take another look, friend," he advised. "You've only seen half of the show."

For a second rider had bobbed over the rise to range alongside the first. This second man was the giant Negro Domingo, who filled a saddle to fullness. Domingo wore range garb, but he now held himself with military stiffness. For a moment the two were starkly sky-lined; then they came forward, the black keeping at the heels of the colonel's horse. When they were near enough, the soldier raised a gauntleted hand in courteous salute and asked, "Who's in charge heah?"

"I am," Brandon said, and identified himself by name. Boxed T brand on both horses, he noticed. It had been too dark to read brands that first night he'd met Domingo.

"I, sir," said the soldier, "am Colonel Templeton. Alan Templeton. At present attached to General Longstreet's command, as is my companion, Captain Israel Domingo, a freeman. I perceive that you're constructing a telegraph line. For whom, may I ask?"

Some whispered warning deep in his mind gave Brandon an inkling of what the proper answer should be and so forged the lie for him. "Our superiors are located in New Orleans," he said.

"New Orleans!" There was the look of the hawk to Templeton, the same fierce eye, the same bold beak. "New Orleans, sir, is in Yankee hands! General Butler holds the city and Farragut's fleet hammers at Vicksburg." He turned quickly to the silent Domingo. "You've deployed our troops properly, Captain? We have this camp completely surrounded?"

Before them the broad sweep of the valley spread, with only that one slight rise breaking vision in this vicinity. There was no place nearby where a body of men might be hidden, yet Domingo said solemnly, "Yo' order been carried out, suh," a note of sadness in his voice.

That sadness drove into Brandon and took the ridiculousness out of the situation and smothered the laughter that had begun building in him. This, then, was the eccentric holding forth in the Valley of the Three Sisters, who had kept Mountain Telegraph's surveyors out, forcing them to choose a longer route to Warlock. Brandon had expected a crazy one of the long-haired, wild-eyed kind. Instead he'd found a courteous man, a man of obvious breeding. Yet this man was mad—so mad that for him time stood still. Nearly two decades after the peace of Appomattox, the war that belonged to the yesterdays remained an actuality to Colonel Alan Templeton. Real as the horse under him and the saber at his side.

What was it Doc King had said in Salish when he, Brandon, had asked about the eccentric of the Three Sisters? "I could tell you a great deal about him. But the person happens to be both my friend and my patient."

And the girl—the one called Miss Ellen, who'd come with this same Israel Domingo to save a trapped Mountain Telegraph man and to ask that man not to enter the Valley of the Three Sisters? The girl who'd had her own reason for her request, a reason which she hadn't cared to put into words. Holt Brandon could see her face in Alan Templeton's, and another riddle was solved. He'd have bet next month's paycheck that she was Templeton's daughter, and he could understand why she hadn't wanted to explain the madness of her father.

Now a lot of things were clear to him, but the problem was no less because he understood. A man stood before him who opposed the telegraph line, and you had to subdue this man with a different weapon from one you'd use against another. You could draw your gun on a Champ McCoy but not against an Alan Templeton, not and own your pride afterward.

"I'm a Texan myself, sir," Brandon said. "And I give you a Confederate's word of honor that this telegraph is a private enterprise, having nothing to do with the war."

"A Texan?" Templeton's lean face remained rigid. "Then why aren't you in uniform? You appear able-bodied. And no enterprise can be considered as having nothing to do with the war as long as there is a war. You've had your say, and I'm not convinced. I perceive that you and your men are not properly armed for combat, and the fact that I came here under a sort of truce stays my hand. I shall return within the week. If I find you and your men still here, I'll have no choice but to order a charge. Do I make myself clear?"

"Now, look—" Brandon began.

"Good day, sir!" Templeton said emphatically.

Behind Templeton, Domingo shook his great head, his eyes sad, his thick lips forming soundless words. In his face was a plea for tolerance, a mute asking for understanding that cooled the temper in Brandon. Now he knew in what coin he was supposed to pay his debt to this giant black, and he nodded slightly.

Templeton saluted stiffly and neck-reined his horse around, and the two went clattering up the rise. At the top they showed briefly against the sky, a Don Quixote in Confederate gray and his gigantic Sancho. And then they were gone.

6

HEART OF NIGHT

When the supper fire had burned low that evening, Brandon called Jake Fargo to his tent. Fargo, tall and stringy, bobbed through the canvas flap and found a seat in the midst of Brandon's gear, folding himself down awkwardly in this close confinement. The tent held, among other things, telegraph instruments and was thus the outer station from which messages were flashed back to Salish. Brandon had been testing to make sure there was no break in the line. He kept fiddling with the key until the job was completed.

"Well, Jake," he asked, "what did you think of the old warrior this afternoon?"

Fargo grunted in his whiskers. Gray as a badger, Fargo. He was a good man when sober, and wise with the years, but something was lacking in him, some driving force that might have made him construction chief if his back trail hadn't been marked by several thousand empty whisky bottles. In each of these Fargo had left some small part of his surety. You could count on him to carry out an order, but only if you blazed the way.

Fargo said now, "The man means business, Holt. But I reckon he's got more bark than bite. His cavalry troop is all in his head, of course, but even a couple men with rifles could give us trouble. Lucky we've been posting guards. The war is just as real to that loony as if it were going on." He gave Brandon a speculative, sidelong glance. "You figuring to change the route back out of the valley, Holt?"

Brandon shook his head. He had entered the Valley of the Three Sisters to string wire, and he had known that some eccentric would try to bar the way. Now he had met the man, but nothing had changed, really. He said, "The thing that worries me is how big a force Templeton has and whether they'd back him in any real play to keep us out. His crew can't be crazy, too, and willing to fight the old war. But if he convinced them that we are trespassers, they might be willing to trouble us."

"What do you figure to do, then?"

"He's got a ranch farther up the valley somewhere. At least he's got a brand, and he must hole up someplace. I'm going to scout his layout tonight, Jake. Likely I'll be back before sunrise. But if I get held up, I want you to keep the crew pushing hard tomorrow."

Fargo asked, "You're riding out soon?"

"Soon as I get saddled. Good night, Jake."

But Fargo didn't move. He had a worry of his own; it showed so plainly on his whiskered face that Brandon asked impatiently, "What is it, man?"

"Pay day was yesterday," Fargo said.

"I know." Brandon's lips drew tight; he had been expecting this, though not quite so soon. "As a matter of fact, Salish reminded me over the wire and was all set to send out the money. I told Sam Whitcomb to hold it in town. There'll be a big payoff at Warlock when the line is finished."

Fargo frowned. "Nothing said about that when the crew signed up."

Brandon turned a hard face toward him. "I'll have no man heading for town for a night of carousing till the line's finished. They can damn well get that straight in their heads. I let them have their fun before this race got hot. Now they can buckle down. And since they can't spend money out here, the company might as well be holding it for them. What's the matter with you, Jake? A big thirst crowding you?"

"It can keep till Warlock," Fargo said. "The boys are muttering, though. Holding the money back is just like putting them on the Injun list. You're making a mistake, Holt."

"My worry," Brandon said and was tired of this.

Fargo said with an old man's temerity and bluntness, "You're a good man, Holt. You push a crew as hard as Creighton did on Western Union, and he beat Overland Telegraph into Salt Lake City after covering twice as much country. But to handle a crew proper, you've got to know what it's like to be a crewman. Mountain Telegraph ain't the whole, complete, and total life of all of us. Was I you, I'd get that payroll up here."

Brandon said, "You handle your own job, Jake, and I'll handle mine."

Fargo shook his head. "Somewhere along your trail, something changed you from a man to a machine. I think it must have been in Texas, when you were a kid. It's no business of mine, Holt, so don't bother snapping at me. But I'd hate to be lonely as you—or so damn certain sure of myself."

Brandon arose. "Is that all, Jake?"

"More than enough, Holt."

"I'll try to be back before sunup," Brandon said. "If I'm late, I'll expect to see poles standing where there aren't any now."

Ten minutes later he rode out of camp. He headed almost directly northwest, driving deeper into the valley, and soon the moon showed and the land lay bright all around. Brighter than he liked, considering that he was on a sneaky mission and didn't want to be seen coming by any guards that Colonel Templeton might have posted. He judged that the old gentleman would have things done up proper and brown in the military manner, with sentinels changed on the hour and a password and all the trimmings. But still it was nothing to laugh about, that peculiar madness of the man.

He shivered involuntarily and couldn't have told whether the reflex came from the thought of Templeton or because of the night air. Summer came damn slow to this high country of Montana, and June was a month of rain, though there'd been little so far. Soon this whole land would be blanketed with summer flowers—columbines and wild geraniums and lupines. Or so a waitress had told him in a Salish restaurant that first week when the crew had worked so close to town that the evening meals were taken across tables. The girl had been mighty excited about the flowers and kind of hungry-looking when she talked about them. Brandon had seen the flowers of all the frontier, from the waxy white bloom of the desert saguaro to the rose-colored petals of the hardy bitterroot. They'd never interested him much, though he reckoned he'd have missed them if they weren't there.

Come to reflect on it, the swing of the seasons had

meant to him only the variations in work. Wintertime a
telegraph man had to roundside and overhaul equipment, unless the country happened to be the kind
where the deep snows held off and let a post-hole digger
get at his doings. Spring spelled rain and wagons mired
in mud; and summer was the good season except for
mosquitoes, if you happened to be working along a
river. Fall meant frost and a hard time getting men to
roll out of their blankets, and some with the wild-goose
strain in them looking south and itching to draw their
pay and be gone. And so one year rolled along after
another, and you could tally them by the wire strung
and the number of new poles standing against the sky.

Well, there was always another line to be put up, and
a new set of problems; and this Montana job had handed
him a corker, all right. This brought his mind back to
Templeton and the mission of tonight. He lifted the
reins and let the piebald gallop awhile, and then he
pulled her down to a walk. The country was growing a
bit rougher, with coulees making long blue lakes of
shadows here and there, and more timber showing,
wind-twisted junipers mostly, looking as if they had the
agonies. He guessed he had put the camp quite a far
piece behind; the stars told him that midnight was past.
He rode on through the heart of night.

Then the land dropped away before him, and at the
foot of the slope the buildings of a ranch sprawled.

He came upon this spectacle so abruptly as to be
startled; and with the moon as bright as it was, he had a
feeling of exposure. To his left he saw a small clump of
junipers, and he headed his mount that way and felt
easier when he got among the trees. From here he
could still see the ranch, and he began to identify the
buildings one by one.

The main house was long and low and made of logs.
Few sawmills in this part of the country, he reckoned;

he'd not seen many frame buildings except in the towns. The barn was big, and the corrals were many. Several outbuildings—these would be blacksmith shop and wagon shed, and a granary, perhaps. The bunkhouse interested him the most, for it, too, was long and low and built of logs. Looked like it could hold from a dozen to twenty men. If that bunkhouse was full, then Templeton kept a sizable crew.

This had to be Boxed T. From this direction Templeton had come, and to this part of the valley he'd returned. Brandon remembered fragments of talk he'd heard in Salish his first week. There'd been some mention of cattle being grazed in the Three Sisters. Farther north, he supposed now, for he'd come upon no stock in this night's riding.

No light showed in any of the buildings below. Brandon dismounted and hunkered upon his heels and spun up a cigarette. Some instinct stayed his hand before he got the match lighted, and he let paper and tobacco drop. He squatted for a long time, studying the ranch and debating whether to go closer. Nothing to be gained by that—he'd wanted to judge the size of the crew, and the bunkhouse had given him a good notion of Boxed T's strength. Likely there'd be a dog or two down there, and maybe a man posted as guard.

His thighs began to ache, and he stood up. He walked forward to the very edge of where the land began dropping away. Part of the edge was rimrock-tipped and precipitous; in other places the land tilted down gently. He stood still in the moonlight and let his eyes rove wide, feeling very small in the immensity of this night and this country. Then an electric shock touched his spine. No more than a quarter of a mile away, a light showed.

Someone with a lantern stood farther along the rim,

to the west. Whoever was there swung the lantern back and forth as a signal.

At once Brandon melted back into the juniper clump. From this cover he stood peering, held by a great curiosity. Time dragged slow feet, and then he thought he detected movement below. He couldn't be sure, and his eyes ached from the effort to separate shadow from substance. Somebody moving down there, leading a horse. Walker and mount got far enough from the buildings to be seen more plainly; the person below rose to saddle. Brandon lifted his eyes and swung his head. The lantern no longer showed.

One person signaling; another coming in answer to that signal.

Brandon looked up at the moon. It moved in the heavens; it moved toward a cloud rack. He waited, wishing he could boot the moon onward; he waited what seemed an endless time, and then the great shadow fell. The piebald nudged Brandon with her head. He said, "Easy, girl," whispering it, and moved again from the junipers, leaving the mare behind. He headed toward where that lantern had swung; he ran in a crouching position and hoped his bootfalls wouldn't betray him. He watched the sky, and when the moon appeared again, he flung himself into a clump of chokecherry bushes near the rim.

Damn scratchy cover, and the ground was rocky beneath his knees. He had to wait longer this time for shadow, and he couldn't risk looking to see where that horseman rode. The giant Domingo? There was a man who'd already proved that he liked night riding. But the rider hadn't looked so large as Domingo. Colonel Templeton? Then he heard the jingle of a bit chain, the creak of saddle leather; and he risked raising himself. A horse humped over the rise perhaps fifty feet from him. The shadow fell and lingered only a short time, and then the moon showed itself again. In the light, he saw Ellen Templeton and another who'd come along the rim leading a horse. That second prowler of the night was Sherm Lucas.

A stiff and angry Lucas who spoke in a harsh voice. "I thought you'd never show up!"

Ellen's voice was remote and toneless. "I saw your first signal an hour ago. I couldn't make up my mind to meet you. When you used the lantern again, I slipped out."

Lucas said impatiently, "I rode away and then decided to give you a second chance. I suppose you haven't made up your mind about the other thing, either."

She said, "I've thought about it. God knows, I've thought about it. But I can't do it, Sherm."

He held the reins in one hand. He slapped these reins across his free hand. "So you'd rather stay with him," he said. "You'd rather waste your life away. You'll look at yourself every morning and you'll be one day older and not one minute happier. Is that your choice, Ellen? You'll dry up like an alkali flat in the sunlight, and you'll be no good for anybody, including yourself. Think, Ellen!"

"He's an old man, Sherm. He's a sick man."

"That big black can take care of him better than you can. Why the devil didn't you wrap that iron box in a slicker and bring it along? We could have ridden away tonight."

She said in a dead voice, "You wouldn't have wanted what you'd have got, Sherm. Not half a girl, with the other half somewhere on the back trail."

He came closer and reached up and touched her. She didn't draw back, nor did she encourage him. His hand lifted to her shoulder, and he drew her down until he could kiss her. His voice changed suddenly—too suddenly—to a soft, pleading tone. "Ellen, how long do you think I can go on waiting?" His voice dropped too low for Brandon to hear, but Ellen's words came clearly.

"Give me more time, Sherm. Just a little more time."

Lucas stepped back from her, and though his face was unreadable to Brandon at such a distance, there was something in the gesture of the man that told Brandon here was one who knew his woman because he knew all women.

Lucas's voice turned harsh again. "I can come and take that box any time I want to run the risk," he said. "You know that. I can crack it open and fill my pockets and ride off. But that's only half of what I'm after. I'm not a cold man, Ellen, so I'm not a patient one. You'd better have your answer ready the next time I swing the lantern."

She said, "Sherm, do you think waiting is easy? Do you think I haven't already started looking at myself in the mirror each morning? It's not that I don't want to come to you. It's only that I can't come free-minded."

"The world is full of girls," he said flatly. He moved away from her and climbed aboard his horse and reined it around. He slapped at his horse with the reins, and she cried out, "Sherm!" and he turned and looked at her. But her shoulders had slumped, and she didn't speak again. Lucas studied her for a long moment. Then he tossed his head impatiently and rode away.

She looked after him, her face blank in the moonlight, and Brandon was glad that he couldn't read her eyes. He had the feeling that he'd seen her naked and so knew the same shame that might have been his if he'd stood watching outside her window, held there too spellbound to move. She brought her horse around and headed toward the rim, and Brandon rose from the bushes.

"Hold up," he called.

She turned in her saddle; her free hand fell and rose, and he saw the glint of moonlight on a drawn gun. She hadn't been wearing a gun that night he'd first met her, but she was wearing one now. This told him much.

He said quickly, "It's me—Brandon!" He took three strides forward with his hands half raised; he got close enough to see recognition on her face.

"Oh!" she said, the single word a long sigh. She swayed in her saddle. He reached her and put up his hand to steady her, but she'd got hold of herself. She put the gun away.

7

WAGON AFLAME

He made a cigarette, wanting something for his hands to do. He had the paper twisted into shape and the match held ready when he remembered the other cigarette and why he hadn't smoked it. He listened hard and heard the distant beat of hoofs that told him Lucas rode far out and away. Lucas might circle about and come back; the game Lucas played with this girl could call for such a feint. He thought, *The hell with him!* and struck the match and got the tobacco fired. A fellow like Lucas made you ashamed of being cut to his shape; he gave you an itch in the knuckles that grew the more you thought about him.

Ellen looked down from her saddle and said, "I can guess what you must think of me."

He drew on the cigarette. "Next time he waves that lantern, why don't you try putting it out with a rifle shot?"

"He's not to blame," she said. "You see, I've been willing enough."

"Except that you've packed a gun. You really don't trust him."

"It's myself I don't trust," she said. "Likely the gun wouldn't have helped."

He made a small gesture with his hands. "Look, you don't have to talk about this."

"There has never been anyone to listen before," she said. "I first met him months ago, when I was riding one day in the hills. He can be charming and gay. He taught me to laugh. I seemed always to run into him after that, and finally he told me who he was. By then I guess it didn't matter. Then we started this signal arrangement. Some night soon I suppose I'll come and ride away with him."

Brandon looked at the glowing end of his cigarette. "Has he ever mentioned a preacher?"

Her face stayed blank. "No," she said. "He hasn't."

"Oh, hell!" Brandon said.

Her steadfastness broke then; she shuddered, and her mouth lost its inflexibility. "I'm twenty-four," she said. "For nineteen years I've mothered my own father through his queer sickness, and for eleven years I've run our ranch. I bought a fancy dress a year ago. I put it on in my room and paraded before a mirror to know how it feels to be gay and carefree. I have never been to a dance or a party, and no man has ever kissed me but Sherm Lucas. I've lived alone and marked my birthdays alone and slept alone. I've not quibbled with what Sherm has so far offered me."

He let the cigarette drop and ground it under his heel. He lifted his eyes to her. He saw her again as femininity in the moonlight, faintly perfumed and soft-breasted and desirable, just as he had the night of their first meeting. But now he knew that the long-buried hunger in him was hers, too, and he could understand how acute her hunger had become. She had been often sad, this one, crying out for someone to recognize that she was woman and ready for awakening. He remembered meeting this girl and another, Gail, and how both had stirred him deeply. But a man didn't trade on a woman's need, and his anger blazed against Sherm Lucas.

"He mentioned an iron box," Brandon said. "What's that got to do with it?"

"It's one my father brought from Kentucky," she said. "He kept it at the bank in Salish for a while. Then he got the queer notion that the Federals were going to invade Salish, so he moved the box to the ranch. The whole range buzzed with talk about that, people making wild guesses as to what valuables the box contained. Sherm Lucas heard the talk."

"Strikes me that he wants the box more than he wants you."

"I suppose," she said. "He's that sure of me. You see how little pride I have left."

"Are you afraid he'll raid the ranch for the box if you don't fetch it to him?"

She shook her head. "I'd like to say I've been stringing along with him to protect the ranch. I think you *want* me to say it, Mr. Brandon. But it wouldn't be quite true. He'll raid the ranch for the box if it comes to that. He's a stubborn man, and a wild one. I've hoped for a better bargain from him, that's all. There's that preacher you mentioned."

Again he had the feeling of seeing her naked, but her honesty made him less ashamed of this than he'd first been. He wanted mightily to reach out to her, but not with his hand. He wanted to say that he understood loneliness and all the needs that had to be denied, and that he, too, had long been held by servitude to another that sometimes rubbed him raw. But he had no words that would not somehow hold a sting, so he said, to cover his awkwardness, "We had visitors today. Your father came to my camp with Domingo."

"Yes," she said. "I know. But you're still not turning back, are you?"

He shook his head. "I'm sorry for him."

She said, "He's got a special reason for hating telegraph wire. Do you remember the storming of Fort Loudon near Knoxville in 1863? General Longstreet ordered the assault, and the men stumbled into telegraph wire strung between stumps. That threw the front ranks into disorder, with Federal cannon sweeping them. It was there that my father's head was creased by the rifle ball that took his memory. I was only a child at the time. But I've heard him fight that telegraph wire many times in his sleep."

"You brought him here to Montana?"

She nodded. "When I was thirteen years old, I talked him into the move. You see, I had to grow up quickly. We sold everything we owned in Kentucky. We got a few cattle here—native stock—and built up the ranch with the help of a small crew. I thought that peaceful surroundings, far from any talk of the war, might work a cure. They haven't."

He glanced down at the dark buildings in the sweep of country below. "Mighty big bunkhouse for a small crew."

"We hoped to grow," she said. "But we've only five men. Six, counting Domingo. He's a West Indian black, a manumitted slave who worked for our family in Kentucky. He was with my father in the army. So were two of the others who are now in our crew. The rest we hired here in Montana—Texas men who'd come up the trail with the first big cattle drives and wanted to stay. I don't think I need to tell you how loyal a cowboy can be, Mr. Brandon."

"But would they attack my camp because of a notion of your father's?"

"They were ready to back him up when he ran your company's surveyors out of the valley months ago. I was terribly worried. For weeks I expected the law to come riding in to investigate. But nothing happened. Today, my father was very grim when he returned from your camp and reported what he'd learned. If he asks the crew to run you out, I think they'll try. After all, Boxed T is private property. Had you thought of that?"

"Yes," he admitted. "I had. Normally Mountain would buy right of way. But how could the company have dickered with a man like your father?"

"I know. And if the crew brings a fight to you, I suppose they'll be outlawed. Does that mean nothing to you?"

He took a moment for thinking before he spoke. "You know young Doc King from Salish?"

"Oh, yes," she said. "He comes out to the place often. He's been treating Dad for the last year or so. Sometimes he thinks he can bring about a cure. But I wonder if he only says that to keep me hoping."

"King is a good man, and I'll bet he's doing his best," Brandon said. "But the point I'm getting at is this. Doc King argues that the railroad and the telegraph will make this country a lot more livable. He's got an eye on tomorrow. I get the notion that it's a kind of religion with him. But there must be a lot of others who think the same. Are such folks to go on living in a wilderness just to suit the fancy of one old man whose clock stopped dead nearly twenty years back?"

It was her turn to be thoughtful. She showed a concerned face in the moonlight; she was a pretty girl in any mood. "I've never looked at it that way," she admitted. "I've spent nearly all my life taking care of him, and that's become habit. Maybe I'm selfish, but his comfort and happiness is my job, and nothing is more important to me. That's why I didn't ride away with Sherm tonight. You see, I hand you back your own ideals and your own stubbornness, Mr. Brandon."

He had to grin. "It's a hell of a fix to be in." He looked over his shoulder into the yonder night, the far expanses. The vastness of the valley lay all around them, night-softened and mysterious and star-dusted. "Did Lucas know it was you who broke up his play when he had me penned in the rocks?"

She shook her head quickly. "He wouldn't forgive me for that. He's not a man who likes to come off second best in anything. And he holds his grudges a long time."

"Then I'm that much deeper in debt to you," he said. "Did you tell Domingo to follow me that night?"

"It was his own idea, but I didn't stop him. The mind of Domingo is deep and dark as a pit. But his loyalty is like sunlight. You'll find that any move Domingo makes is always somehow concerned with Colonel Templeton's well-being."

He looked up at the stars and read the time by them. He was mildly astonished at how late it had become. "I'll have to hump to make it back to camp by sunrise," he said. He glanced toward the junipers. "My horse is over yonder."

She lifted her reins. He looked at her; she was less a mystery now, and so nearer to him. She said, "I've told you more about myself than I've told any other person. I wonder why."

"I don't know," he said. "I hope I've helped you."

"Yes," she said thoughtfully. "You really do hope that, don't you? You're a strange mixture, Mr. Brandon. I wish that Mountain Telegraph wasn't always first with you."

He said, "My name is Holt. Good night, Ellen."

"Good night, Holt." She turned her horse about. "Till we meet again."

When? he wondered. *And how will it come about?* And he remembered the willful madness of Colonel Templeton.

He watched her go down the slope. He had once judged her to be mature beyond her years, a girl with wisdom and courage. He'd seen these traits in her again tonight, and seen, too, that she was human, frail with the flesh's frailness. He wished her well and saw her grow smaller with distance as she picked a careful way toward the ranch buildings. He turned to the junipers where the piebald waited; and in the far hills a coyote lifted its voice in loneliness, the sound drifting across the silence and the night. He shuddered in spite of himself.

He rode into his camp in the darkness before dawn and was challenged by his own sentry before he was allowed to pass. He thought in the wooden way of a man too tired for complete clarity that he would have to ask Sam Whitcomb for more men. The guards should be doubled, now that the threat of attack from Boxed T hung over the camp. You couldn't break up your men's sleep with sentry duty and expect to wring a day's work out of them afterward. Trouble was, though, you couldn't dredge up crewmen from the back rooms of saloons, either. The job called for special skill. But getting new men would be Sam's problem, and Sam had solved it before. He'd wire Sam about it, come daylight.

All he wanted to do now was sleep. He'd ridden southward with the remembrance of Ellen Templeton strong in him, and with the thought of Sherm Lucas and Colonel Templeton, too. Danger in both directions now. This much he'd learned from the night's riding. Boxed T's crew was not large, but it would likely turn its guns against Mountain Telegraph if the order came.

Had to get to sleep, he reminded himself. Deep, woolly sleep was the ticket. Hours of it. Jake Fargo could order out the crew in the morning while the construction chief slept. He groped his way to the tent that Fargo shared with three others; he would tell Jake to take over at daybreak. But Fargo was not in his blankets. Brandon felt around till he was sure of this, and his angry thought was: *He's gone to Salish, damn him!* Fargo's claim to hobbling his great thirst till they reached Warlock had been so much talk.

He didn't wake the others; they needed their sleep. He found his way in the curdled blackness to his own tent, and he knew as soon as he'd bobbed through the flap that someone was inside. A sense of danger touched his spine for a moment and was gone, for he heard deep snoring.

He found a lantern and got it alight and saw Jake Fargo sprawled out upon the blankets. Jake looked like a dead one, but he was snoring. Beside Fargo's outflung hand lay a quart whisky bottle. No need to look to tell that it was empty.

Brandon kneeled by Fargo and got hold of the man's shoulders and shook him hard. His anger was so great as to be beyond anger. He knew instead a numb feeling of despair as though there were no trust left anywhere, no surety. The reek of liquor was strong in his nose, and his shadow did a silly dance on the canvas. Fargo mumbled wild words and batted aimlessly at Brandon's arm. Fargo opened his eyes and blinked in the lantern light; his eyes were empty of understanding.

"Where did you get it?" Brandon demanded.

"Go 'way," Fargo said and tried to wrench free of Brandon's grip and roll over.

"Where did you get it?" Brandon insisted. "The only bottle I had here I took with me nearly two weeks ago."

"Eh? The bottle? Halliday."

"Halliday brought you whisky?"

"Fine man, Halliday. Returning favor. Helped him learn how to telegraph. Brought me whole quart. Yesterday. No, day before yesterday."

Now how the hell had that been, Brandon wondered. Then he remembered that he'd been up ahead with the post-hole diggers when Halliday had first driven his buggy into camp. That must have been when Halliday had passed over the bottle to Jake. Now Brandon's anger had a way of spending itself, and he turned to the telegraph key and jiggled it fiercely, trying to raise Salish. No response there. But divisional headquarters might well be deserted at this useless hour, the night operator busy at something else or gone to bed. Brandon reached for Fargo and shook him again. "Get to your own tent, Jake."

Fargo protested in a jumble of words but at last crawled toward the flap. "You're making a mish—a mistake, Holt. Can't treat men like they wash on the Injun list and get work out of 'em. When you gonna learn that?"

"Get out of here!" Brandon snapped and blew out the lantern.

He got his boots off and his belt laid aside and crawled into the rumpled blankets where Fargo had lain. He'd have thanked Jake to have done his drinking elsewhere. Damned if a man couldn't get a cheap drunk out of the very air of this tent! But he couldn't let that keep him from sleep; he would get only a couple of hours and then he would have to be up and rousing the crew. He let his rage grow white against Halliday, and then slumber overtook him. He'd willed himself to wake at the usual time, and shortly he was moving about in the first gray of morning. Another day had begun.

He got the post-hole diggers strung out and the rest of the crew at their duties; he was a morose man at this, with no juice of kindness in him. He returned to his tent and opened the line to Salish. He raised divisional headquarters and got Sam Whitcomb at the other end. Brandon tapped quickly: T-E-L-L H-A-L-L-I-D-A-Y I-F H-E B-R-I-N-G-S M-O-R-E W-H-I-S-K-Y T-O C-A-M-P I W-I-L-L B-R-E-A-K T-H-E B-O-T-T-L-E O-V-E-R H-I-S H-E-A-D.

Whitcomb's reply came at once. K-N-O-W N-O-T-H-I-N-G A-B-O-U-T T-H-I-S B-U-T W-I-L-L C-H-E-C-K. It was as though Sam had sent a frown of puzzlement with the dots and dashes.

Within half an hour the set began clattering, and Brandon spelled out the message. Halliday himself was wiring; Brandon recognized the unpracticed hand. I-N-D-E-B-T-E-D T-O F-A-R-G-O F-O-R F-A-V-O-R D-I-D N-O-T K-N-O-W M-A-N I-S B-O-T-T-L-E F-I-G-H-T-E-R W-H-I-T-C-O-M-B H-A-S E-X-P-L-A-I-N-E-D E-X-T-R-E-M-E-L-Y S-O-R-R-Y.

Brandon shook his head and went back to supervise his crew. Afterward he remembered that he'd meant to ask Sam for more men. Well, he'd do that later.

Fargo showed from his tent at noon, hard-used and ugly and not quite able to meet Brandon's eye. Fargo said, "There's just one thing that needs to be got straight, Holt. Halliday didn't know I'd burn up that whole quart in one night. If you've got to give somebody hell, give it to me."

"Get to work, Jake," Brandon said bluntly and turned away from the man.

Fargo said, "Just a minute, Holt," and even his whiskers looked truculent. "I don't know all that I did last night or all that I said, but I can guess, because I know what I was thinking about. I had that quart night before last, remember. But I didn't tap it. Half of what made me finally open it was defiance. It's something for you to think about. You've held back the payroll because you don't trust any of us to stay on the job if our pockets are jingling. When you put it to a man that he can't have something, he's likely to try to show you that he bigawd can!"

Brandon felt his temper surge, but he kept a tight hold on it. "There's a lot I could say to you, Jake, that I'm not saying. I'm trying to remember all the camps we shared together. Don't needle me any more than you already have. Now get to work."

He walked away from Fargo and tried dismissing the man from his mind, not wanting his temper to grow beyond holding. He was too tired to permit himself anger, and he knew it. He needed to crawl back into his blankets, but there was wire to be strung. He saw poles go up that afternoon and found a sour satisfaction in the progress made. He got Whitcomb on the wire again and asked about more men, and Sam promised to see what he could do. Sam had a question, too. Had Gail been along with Halliday the other day?

Brandon wired him no. Whitcomb admitted worry. The girl had been seeing a lot of Halliday of late.

Brandon returned to his camp. He had a crazy man ready to make war on the camp, and he had his ablest assistant whisky-soaked and ready to mutiny. Sam Whitcomb could damn well do all the worrying about his willful daughter. Yet there was a contagion in Whitcomb's fear.

Brandon pushed the crew till suppertime and ate morosely with them. He debated about a night shift and decided against it. He named three men to sentinel duty, and while the crew still squatted around the fire, he crawled into his tent. He flung himself down, not even removing his boots, and was lying soaked in sleep when the staccato barking of guns dragged him alive.

At first this commotion was so unreal as perhaps to be part of dreaming, and then he knew better. Beyond the canvas the wild shouts of men, the thud of running boots, the continued beat of gunfire was too real to be denied. He thought, *Templeton!* and remembered that the week wasn't up. But time had no real meaning to Templeton. He came hurrying out of the tent and saw that the teamster's wagon was afire. Only coal oil, liberally sloshed, could make a blaze as bright as that.

Jake Fargo stumbled past him, shouting orders at the crew. Fargo saw him and said from the corner of his mouth, "They snuck close enough to set the wagon ablaze. Now they're out there throwing lead to keep us from fighting the fire."

Brandon saw them then, a half dozen or more riders who were circling the camp Indian-fashion, firing steadily. In the first starlight he saw them and recognized the biggest one, and with them was Champ McCoy. This was McCoy's method, old and familiar.

The sentries! Brandon wondered wildly. What the hell had the sentries been doing? Then he realized he'd been asleep only a short while and that the sentries, who usually began guard duty when the crew rolled into blankets, had not yet gone to their posts. Brandon cursed. He'd got himself honed for the danger from Boxed T and grown careless of this other menace. And now it was here.

8

THE LONG SHADOW

Close by Brandon a gun began a steady hammering, and he saw one of the post-hole diggers down on his knee, working a Winchester. The fellow chose no target; he merely fired blindly and pumped the lever and fired again, like a machine set in motion. Jake Fargo's was a big voice in the night; Fargo seemed to be every-where. "Aim before you shoot!" Fargo shouted, but the post-hole digger showed a stunned face in the wash of the firelight.

Brandon stood spraddle-legged, his gun in his hand and the sweat of excitement cold on his skin. Around him the camp had become chaos, the rope-corralled horses rearing and pitching, men scurrying every which direction, and that wagon blazing brightly, mak-ing the scene something out of a nightmare. With the firelight in his eyes, the outer darkness was all the thicker, but he could make out movement. He tried a shot at the biggest raider, the one he believed to be Champ McCoy.

Not too big a force attacking. Brandon tried counting again, and again he judged that only seven or eight circled the camp. His own force was greater, but his crew stood exposed in the firelight. That was the pinch.

Brandon shouted, "Wheel up the water barrels! Get that fire out!"

The teamster had been filling barrels at the nearest creek each day, and the barrels stood here and there about the camp. Brandon ran to one and began tussling with it. Several of the crew had flung themselves be-hind a barricade of piled telegraph poles. A man left this protection to lend Brandon a hand, and they worked the barrel toward the blazing wagon. Brandon found a bucket and began sloshing the wagon. A bullet gouged dirt near his feet, and from the outer darkness came the high, strident yell of one of the raiders.

"Damn close!" Brandon's helper said.

Brandon grunted and worked on. A bullet clanged against the bucket he held, the impact stinging his hands. He discarded the bucket as useless, but he and his helper had now lowered the contents of the barrel by half.

"Give it a heave," Brandon ordered.

They lifted the barrel and tossed the water at the flames, moving so close to the wagon that Brandon felt the heat against his face and wondered if he still had eyebrows. Others were wheeling up water barrels; they spilled one over in their haste. But the wagon was soon being drenched from all sides; smoke rose, and steam, and became stifling, and the smell of charred wood was strong. In another ten minutes the blaze was out, and only stars lighted the camp. But death still moved in the night, for the raiders rode their endless circle.

Again Brandon looked about him. Here and there guns winked close by, telling him where his own men were stationed. And from the outer darkness guns replied. Brandon marked a gun flash, and making allowance for the direction the raider was heading and the speed at which he galloped, he fired at the emptiness where he hoped the man might be. He had the feeling that he missed.

And then, suddenly, the fight was over.

The raiders, turning tail, were scattering to the four winds, their defiant jeers drifting back. Cooler hands among the Mountain crew threw gear onto horses, and three or four riders went roaring out of camp. As well chase the wind, Brandon thought, but he let them go. The guerrilla tactics Champ McCoy had tonight displayed were easy enough to savvy, especially when you had had a taste of them before. The surprise attack had been intended to throw the camp into panic; the blazing wagon was to have further terrorized the crew. Hit hard and run fast. That had been the notion; and now McCoy and Lucas and the others were running.

Near where Brandon stood, someone groaned. Brandon saw a huddled shape, a seated man with his knees drawn up to his chin. "Who is it?" Brandon asked.

"Me—Pete," one of the wire stringers said. His voice was sharp with pain. "I got nicked."

"Bad?"

"In the arm. No bones broken."

"Spit tobacco juice on the wound and wrap it with your bandanna," Brandon advised. "Don't worry. We'll get you fixed up soon."

He went striding toward his tent and groped for the telegraph key and at once raised the night operator at Salish. Brandon breathed easier then; he'd feared that the line might be cut, but McCoy hadn't bothered. McCoy had known that help couldn't be got from Salish before the attack was over. Brandon's message was short. C-A-M-P S-H-O-T U-P S-O-M-E W-O-U-N-D-E-D F-I-N-D D-O-C-K-I-N-G A-N-D S-E-N-D H-I-M F-A-S-T.

He got his acknowledgment and left the tent. Around him the camp lay silent; to the far south he thought he heard the drumbeat of hoofs, but that might be an echo out of imagination. He saw his crew, a close knot of men in the starlight held quiet in the backwash of danger endured. He asked, "How about Pete?"

"I've got a bandage on him," the cook said.

"Anybody else hurt?"

"Two others. They'll make out."

"Do the best you can with them," Brandon said. "I've got Doc King coming."

Now there was nothing to do but wait, and time became a rasp on his nerves. He looked about for Fargo and found that he'd been one of those who'd mounted and given the raiders a chase. He named another man to sentry duty and so had two posted to the north of camp, two to the south. He fretted about those who'd ridden out and not returned. Fargo was a good man when the chips were down; Brandon had that to remember. Fargo had made one mistake the other night, but the whisky was gone, and Fargo was trying hard to redeem himself. He hoped that wouldn't make for recklessness in Jake.

He inspected the wounded and found them in fair shape, though one was showing fever. You could have fried an egg on that fellow's forehead. Brandon let a small fire be lighted; sleeplessness held the camp, and the men sat morosely before their tents. Sam Whitcomb, aroused by the night operator at Salish, wired for details of the attack, and Brandon gave them. To Sam, also, it was an old story; only the name on the map was different. After that, Brandon tried getting some sleep.

He was not sure that he really slept, but he did sprawl out on his blankets, and at times he dozed a bit. Near morning he was brought alert by hearing one of the sentries raise his voice in challenge. Brandon groped out of the tent. Doc King rode into camp on a lathered horse.

"So now I start earning my pay," King said, smiling, but his poet's face was gray with strain.

Brandon took him to the wounded and watched while King worked, standing fascinated by the swift and certain play of King's slender hands. A good man at his job, young Jonathan King. He soothed his patients down with a few soft words as he went about probing for lead. He kept the cook hustling hot water or holding a lantern just so; but before King had finished with his second patient, the murk of early morning was in the camp, and soon the lantern wasn't needed.

Brandon came out into the openness and cupped his hands to his mouth. "Dawn's here, boys!" he shouted. "Roll out!"

They spilled from the tents and had their breakfast and got to their appointed tasks. The teamster looked at his burned wagon and shook his head, but Brandon said, "It's got wheels under it, mister. And the tongue didn't burn. New equipment will be coming up from Salish, but you'll have to make this work meanwhile. Get at it."

The teamster turned a surly face Brandon's way. "So it's fight half the night and then work all day with a wagon that's ready to bust in the middle! And to top it off, we wait till you're good and ready to give us our pay!"

Brandon said, "Your pay's safe," and put his back to the man and strode away. Half an hour later, when the post-hole diggers were strung out in a grumbling line, Brandon was approached by Doc King and the two of them went to Brandon's tent.

King looked tired, but the joy of work performed showed on him. His was a spirit that fed and fattened on work. "That fellow Pete, the one with the wounded arm, will be back on the job in a couple of days," he reported. "The man with the hurt shoulder will get along all right, too. But the fever case is going to need watching. You'd better send him to Salish for a while."

Brandon made a fist out of his hand. Men out of commission meant men that had to be replaced, with no one to do their chores meanwhile. Truly, Champ McCoy had tallied the way he'd intended last night. A job added up to men and time, pitted against miles and terrain; and when you had your crew worn raw by a night like last night, and some not able to work, you had Warlock shoved just that much farther away. You got to feeling that everything in the world was an annoyance and that you dragged a load about that made you slow-footed while the race was run.

He looked at King. "I appreciate your getting up here so fast, Doc."

King said, "I know the country pretty well. I have a lot of night calls."

Brandon's mind shunted to the night before last. "Some that take you as far as Boxed T?"

Worry shadowed King's young face. "You're into the Three Sisters now. I suppose that means you've met the colonel. I tried to stop you, Brandon. But you've still got that square jaw."

Brandon said, "Boxed T needs more than a doctor. It needs a man to take over. But you know that already. Your face gives you away, Doc. I think more than the colonel interests you up there."

King shook his head. "All I mean to her is the hope that someday her father may be cured."

"Ah," Brandon said.

"There's a man who sometimes swings a lantern at night, Brandon." King's face stiffened. "She comes to meet him when he does. I saw them the first time by the merest happenstance; I confess to having spied on them since. What is it about worthless men that makes them so attractive to women?"

"I haven't got the answer to that one, Doc."

King said, "Every man to his own troubles. I don't know why I burden you with mine."

Brandon had to grin. "Because you've got to speak to somebody or bust. You've kept this locked up inside you too long." He thought of Ellen, who'd also needed to talk.

King let his hands lie idle in his lap. He looked at them and was a man turned forlorn by his own thinking. "Physician, heal thyself, eh?"

"Something of the sort," Brandon said. "You set a great store by the future. You'd do well to think of more than what's coming to a town and a range. You've got a few tomorrows ahead of you yourself."

King said, "I've already told you. I mean nothing to her but a hope for her father."

Outside, a shout was raised, and it brought Brandon from the tent on the bound. His nerves were getting edgy, he knew—too edgy. It was Fargo who'd ridden in,

Fargo and the three others who'd gone with him. Jake's whiskery face puckered with an ill-humored smile. "They're far gone," he said. "It was Champ McCoy, all right. I got close enough to be sure of that. He'd lie out of it in a court, though." He swung from the saddle, making an awkward dismount; pain showed on his face.

"You're hurt," Brandon said.

"I likewise got close enough to get singed," Fargo admitted. "A flesh wound in my shoulder."

"More work for you, Doc," Brandon said to King, who had followed him from the tent. Brandon looked at the others who had ridden with Fargo. "If you fellows have whole hides, go have the cook rustle you something to eat. Then there's work waiting yonder."

They helped Fargo into Brandon's tent and seated him on the blankets. King went to work on him at once. With his shirt cut away and his torso bared, Fargo showed an expanse of body amazingly white in contrast to his sun-dyed face. He winced as King swabbed an ugly gash across his shoulder. "You still holding up the payroll, Holt?" he asked.

Brandon said wearily, "Haven't any of you got anything on your minds but that?"

Fargo said, "I guess I'm going to have to come out and tell you, Holt. It's been whispered around that Mountain overstretched its credit and can't pay. A story like that grows. But a little money spread around this camp would make a lie out of it. *Ouch!* Doc, can you go a little easier?"

Brandon said, "I thought you were a tough one. You'd think this was the first wound you ever had."

"The fifth for Mountain Telegraph," Fargo said. "The others don't count. How about that payroll, Holt?"

Brandon turned to the telegraph key. He knew what message he was going to send, and he knew his reason for sending it was not that there was talk in camp that had to be stilled. Something else had proved stronger than his own stubbornness, something that lay in Jake Fargo's screwed-tight face as King worked at the wound, something that had come out of a night of danger shared once more with his crew. But chiefly it was Jake. The message ran: S-E-N-D P-A-Y-R-O-L-L A-T O-N-C-E.

Whitcomb was at the other end and replied promptly. H-A-L-L-I-D-A-Y O-N R-O-A-D N-O-W W-I-T-H P-A-Y-R-O-L-L M-E-A-N-T T-O S-E-N-D M-O-N-E-Y Y-E-S-T-E-R-D-A-Y P-E-R Y-O-U-R R-E-Q-U-E-S-T O-F N-I-G-H-T B-E-F-O-R-E S-O-R-R-Y A-B-O-U-T D-E-L-A-Y.

Brandon stared at Fargo. "Did you get that?"

"Hell, I could read Morse before you could, Holt."

Brandon said hotly, "Why, you damn drunken—"

Fargo held up a hand. "Whoa, Holt. I told you I couldn't remember all I said and did that night. Somewhere in the middle of that bottle, I must have come across the notion that it would be a good idea to put your name at the end of a message. Where's the harm, since you want the payroll anyway?"

Brandon laughed in spite of himself, and laughing, was done with anger. "It must have been the night operator who got your message. Sam would have known it was you and guessed that you were drunk."

King looked up from his work in surprise. "How's that?"

"A man's touch on the key is as recognizable as his voice," Brandon explained. "Whitcomb knows my touch, and he knows Jake's. Anyway, we've sure got a payroll coming." But there was a core of worry for him in this moment, and he at once touched it. "Halliday," he mused. "I wish Sam could have found somebody else for the delivery job."

Fargo's eyes brightened with interest. "You're thinking of McCoy's outfit heading south, with Halliday coming up from that direction? Is that it? Soon as this man gets finished with me, I'll ride down and meet Halliday."

Brandon said, "About all you'll be good for the next couple of days is to sit on a rock and yell orders at the crew. You can start doing that as soon as you get your shirt back on. I'll ride south myself." He glanced at King. "Will you be coming, Doc?"

King said, "Later. I want to look in on that fever case again."

Brandon went out and saddled the piebald. He thought again that he was getting too edgy, yet the facts were there, bold as a lodgepole pine on the sky line. Halliday might indeed drive right into the arms of Lucas and McCoy and those other raiders of last night. Brandon rode out of camp with that worry on him; worry was a long shadow that stretched from Salish to the Valley of the Three Sisters. He cut due south, keeping the telegraph line in view.

Thus he came out of the valley and onto the plain that lifted gently upward from Salish to the folding hills that hemmed the valley. He saw the remembered places where the camp had been and marked his passage by the recollection of days of work that were done. He told himself this was a fool's mission; he might better be superintending his men. But he couldn't be sure. He felt possessed by small frettings and small fears.

The camp a few miles behind him, he came upon a wagon road that ran north out of Salish before it bent westward, and he followed the road, knowing that Halliday would come over it. He veered away from the telegraph line and so found himself in a primitive expanse where the land rose and fell and small, rocky hills hid the horizons. Near here he had been ambushed by Lucas and hoisted to safety by Ellen and Domingo.

Noon came and passed, and he supposed he had covered about a third of the distance to town. Shortly he saw Halliday's buggy.

It stood nearly motionless and just off the road; the horse had fallen to cropping. The buggy looked empty. Spurring closer, Brandon found it was indeed empty. He felt suddenly as though he'd been kicked in the belly. He dismounted and tied the piebald behind the buggy and climbed to the seat. He picked up the reins and wheeled the buggy around and sent it south along the road at a fast clip.

Within the next mile, he found Halliday. The man was seated on a rock beside the road, his head in his hands, his shoulders bowed. He slumped shapeless as a sack of grain. He lifted a startled face as Brandon rode up, and he said in an explosive gust of sound, "Thank God!" His hair was tousled, and his clothes looked as though he'd gone on a hard romp in them.

Brandon said, "Lucas and McCoy, eh?"

Halliday nodded. "McCoy's the only one I knew by sight. There were seven or eight of them."

"They got the payroll, of course."

"And Gail."

This hit Brandon harder than had finding the buggy empty. "Gail—"

"She insisted on coming along. They took her with them." He pointed to the west where far hills lifted. "They rode off in that direction."

Brandon looked toward the hills. Clear to him then came the remembrance of that night in Sam Whitcomb's private car when Lucas and McCoy had entered masked and armed. He'd pondered about that wild play since, not understanding what had prompted the pair. But now he knew. Lucas and McCoy had been given a

second chance and had seized it. This time they'd succeeded in kidnapping Gail and so put Sam Whitcomb at
their mercy.

9

VOODOO

First there'd been fear, and now anger came. The one
was mixed with the other and left Brandon feather-
bellied and hard-fisted; and because he needed something to do, he leaped out and walked to the rear of the
buggy, untied the piebald, and stepped up to saddle. He
looked at the shapeless bulk of Halliday and judged that
the man had been no more than shaken up. He remembered the whisky bottle that had been passed over to
Jake Fargo. Halliday was to have got a piece of
Brandon's mind for that, the next time they met. The
whisky didn't seem important now, but Brandon remembered an earlier matter and couldn't keep from
asking, "You still believe Consolidated wouldn't stoop to
rough play?"

Halliday's face turned redder with anger. "Do you
have to rub that in, Brandon? I've had a bad enough
time this last hour."

"No bones broken, I'd judge. Do you think you can
climb into the buggy?"

Halliday came to an unsteady stand. He was like a
bear ringed by hunters, not knowing where to charge.
He moved his stout shoulders and pushed back his hair
with the heels of his hands and stepped toward the
buggy. "I can manage," he said. "One of them clouted
me hard when I put up a fight."

Brandon looked across the land. "You're a little
nearer the camp than you are to Salish. Take the buggy

on north. You'll probably meet Doc King on the road. But get Whitcomb on the wire and tell him what's happened. I'd cut in from the line, but I didn't fetch climbers or any equipment."

Halliday asked, "Where are you going?"

"After her, of course."

Halliday's face turned hard. "Give me your horse and gun. You take the buggy. Man, she's engaged to me!"

"That was a while back."

"No, we've become engaged again."

This was news to Brandon, and possibly it would be news to Sam Whitcomb, too. Brandon said bluntly, "It isn't going to matter who gets the medal. Don't you see why they've taken her? It's a way of putting Sam Whitcomb over a barrel. They'll force him to meet their terms, which will probably mean forfeiting the Warlock job if he wants her safe, or else they'll expect him to take the whole crew and go stampeding through the hills. Either way, they win. On top of that, they've picked up a payroll that's needed. I've got to cut their sign while it's fresh. It's not your kind of job, mister."

Truculence again showed on Halliday, and it was Brandon's thought that they were once more rubbing each other wrong. Halliday took a step toward the buggy and steadied himself by leaning against a wheel. He climbed to the seat. "You're right, Brandon," he said. "It's too important a matter to be trusted to a greenhorn. I'll get on to camp." Something crossed his face that turned him into a scared man, and he asked, "You don't think they'll harm her?"

"She's too valuable for that," Brandon said, but he wasn't sure.

Halliday said, "Good luck, Brandon."

Brandon neck-reined his mount around and lifted his hand in farewell. And then, because a habit of thinking was strong in him, he said, "You tell Jake Fargo to keep the crew at work. Be sure, now. They don't have to stand around waiting to see how this turns out."

Halliday nodded. "I'll tell him."

Brandon faced west. "They rode off in that direction," Halliday had said. A nice chunk of country to comb, Brandon thought ruefully. It only stretched as far as the big sea! But he looked toward the hills and knew the trail would lead into them. All you had to do was put yourself in Champ McCoy's boots, and he knew McCoy as the tree knows the wind that blows against it. A place to hole up is what McCoy would be hunting. A place where a man could sit on a stump and chuckle at the thought of Mountain's crew spending its strength and its time in wild skallyhooting. A place from which terms could be sent to Sam Whitcomb. And Sherm Lucas, an old hand hereabouts, would know such a place.

In these first miles, the spoor was easily followed. Broad sign showed that many riders had passed this way, striking toward the hills at a slant that was as much north as it was west. Far ahead, Brandon thought he could make out the raised dust of passage, though he wasn't sure, and his eyes tired from squinting. He rode at a high gallop for a way, held the piebald down to a walk or a trot, galloped again. June's heat lay thick upon the land, but clouds built above the hills, and rain was in the making. Rain would wash away sign; he hoped the rain would hold off.

Soon the afternoon was nearly spent; the westering sun gave the sage long shadows, and the grass lay like an emerald lake across which Brandon beat his endless way. Occasionally he came upon heaped buffalo bones, and once he saw an antelope on a ridge.

In the shadow of the hills, he found a creek. The land had turned rockier and coulee-riven, and sometimes the trail of Lucas and his men faded out. Brandon began following the creek, which spilled down from the hills.

Lucas would want to camp by water, and thus the creek might lead him to Lucas, though that was a gamble. These hills were likely crisscrossed with creeks, all of them swollen at this season when the high snows melted. The trail climbed through barren slopes to the first pine and became then a faint spoor made by wandering game. The trail clung close to the creek and moved upward in long loops and short ones, these switchbacks climbing, always climbing.

The first chill came with sundown; this country cooled off fast. Presently Brandon came into a mountain meadow and in the last of the light looked for sign. Bent grass and the fresh and smoking droppings of a horse told him that riders had passed this way and not very long before.

He paused here long enough to build up a smoke and give his situation brief consideration. He'd fetched no food and no blanket but the one under his saddle; therefore his hope lay in a quick finish to all this. He listened sharply and thought he heard the crashing of horses along a timbered trail, but the sound was both remote and hard to place. He was growing hungry, and he was tired, and his mood was gray. Not liking this bold stand in openness, he pushed on across the meadow. There was always the chance that Lucas had set someone to trailing behind.

He rode into timber again and followed another game trail upward until he came upon a promontory that gave him a look at the country below. It spread gray and endless in the half-light; he could see a last glint of sun on the distant telegraph line and wondered what messages sped back and forth between the camp and Salish. He felt sorry for Sam Whitcomb, knowing how the news would hit Sam. He could see all the country he'd crossed since leaving Halliday, and it struck him that if Lucas and his men had looked back from here, they might have seen him, Brandon, when he was on the flats below. But he remembered how fresh the sign had been and judged that Lucas had not been that far ahead of him.

The darkness came like a lamp blown out. He moved on through this darkness, letting the piebald pick her way; he listened always for the racket of the creek. Starlight came and got itself tangled in the treetops and was lost; the moon showed. Something glided overhead with a whoosh of wings; something big and solid as a bear lumbered in the underbrush, and the piebald snorted. The night spoke with many voices, and Brandon harkened to them all.

Presently he came into another of those mountain meadows and here he debated, then stepped down from his saddle. He had put himself on a mission that had to wait till morning, and he knew it. He could cut no further sign tonight and so would only spend himself in futile search. No sense in groping blindly along. He left the piebald saddled but loosened the cinch; he led the mare to the creek and let her drink. He scooped up a mouthful for himself and splashed water over his face. He was a tired man and his thoughts were wooden, and the chill drove at him. He wondered about risking a fire. He bundled up some pine boughs and laid them at the edge of the meadow, but still he was uncertain.

A voice said then, out of darkness, "Safe to light it, suh."

Brandon leaped sideways, his motion having no mind behind it, and he got his gun into his hand. This, too, was instinct, for in the midst of drawing, recognition of that voice came to him. He peered hard in the curdled darkness and found a giant form, and he said with relief, "Ah, Domingo!"

The great body crouched, and a match sprang to life. Domingo, squatting on his heels, cupped the match and held it to the pyramid of pine boughs, then fanned the tiny blaze with his sombrero. He stood up; he showed white teeth in the night. Still smiling, he faded backward and presently returned, leading his horse. Brandon saw that a Winchester rode in a saddle scabbard. From his gear, Domingo produced a coffeepot and a frying pan and went silently about putting these to use.

"Here," Domingo said when the time came and passed bacon and coffee to Brandon.

Brandon said, "You've found a man who's glad to eat what's set before him." He put the food away fast and stretched himself out by the fire. He made up a cigarette and plucked a brand from the fire to light it. He had now a sense of well-being and comfort and surety. He looked at Domingo, who showed a black, placid face. Brandon asked, "How long were you behind me?"

"I've been riding the hills, suh," Domingo said. "Watched a slew of riders from a point. Pretty soon I saw you. Since dark I've been hunting you."

"You know these hills well?"

Domingo nodded. "Better than most. Sweet-lonesome up here. From the high places I see far."

"Could you lead me to Lucas and his outfit?"

Domingo shrugged. "Reckon."

Brandon said, "There's a girl with them. Packed away against her will."

Again Domingo nodded. He seemed like a great, overgrown child trying to make up his mind whether a game was worth playing. "Only two of us," he said at last. "Quite a slew of them. You want that kind of fight?"

"The sooner the better," Brandon said and remembered Halliday's fear.

Domingo arose, and Brandon, too, would have come to his feet, thinking they were leaving, but Domingo motioned him to remain seated. The giant black moved to his horse. He returned with something in his hand.

Seating himself cross-legged before the fire, he closed his eyes and at once his body became tense. Brandon saw that he held a shapeless piece of black wax in his hand. Domingo spoke to himself in a low mumble; the snatches of words were in a tongue strange to Brandon; the Negro's transfixed look made Brandon's skin prickle. He wanted to get away from these queer doings. Domingo began to twitch and shake. He kneaded the wax, and Brandon saw the stuff take the crude shape of a human figure.

Now Domingo fumbled at his boot top and drew from it a bowie knife. With this he pricked his forearm until a drop of blood stood out, bright in the firelight. Pressing the wax figure against his arm, Domingo then laid the figure near the edge of the fire. Brandon felt as though he were choking; hc felt boxed in and wooden-legged. He watched fascinated as the wax began to melt. Soon it was only a shapelessness again. Domingo ceased his rocking and crooning and opened his eyes.

"What the hell is this?" Brandon demanded hoarsely.

"Voodoo," Domingo said. "My mother was a *cunjer*. Sometimes I got the power. Sometimes not. Maybe I take away a man's strength tonight. Lucas's."

Brandon shook his head. The sweat lay cold on his skin, and he remembered that at their first meeting this giant Negro had seemed to him like a black panther. Now the man was something so utterly primitive as to be beyond naming. But Domingo smiled and was thus transformed to a friendly child in the firelight. He arose and beckoned to Brandon.

Within a few minutes they had the fire out and were riding the night, Domingo leading the way. Brandon, dimly able to make out that broad back ahead of him, knew this man as a strange one but a self-sufficient one. He felt armored by that self-sufficiency. Still he remembered what Ellen Templeton had said just two nights back about this black man. "You'll find that any move Domingo makes is always somehow concerned with Colonel Templeton's well-being." Yet here was Domingo leading the way to Sherm Lucas's hideout and asking no favor in return.

In another mountain meadow where the starlight reached and there was room to ride two abreast, Brandon pulled up beside Domingo. "There's something I've got to know," Brandon said. "Come tomorrow, what do I owe you for tonight?"

Domingo shrugged. "Yo' make your own answer to that, white man."

"I'm putting a telegraph line through the Three Sisters," Brandon reminded him.

"Tonight we hate the same man, so we fight him together," Domingo said.

Brandon caught the undercurrent of anger in Domingo's voice, and he thought: *He knows about that swung lantern and how she goes to meet him.* He said, "Just one more thing. I can understand why you hate anyone who might give the old man trouble, or the girl. But why would you fight a crazy man's war for him?"

Domingo said softly, "You mean shooting at the surveyors?"

"That and whatever's to come. Why risk trouble just because of a notion of his?"

Domingo said very solemnly, "He made me captain, suh."

"In the war? Ellen told me you were with him."

"That was General Lee's army, not Colonel Templeton's. The colonel doing his own generalin' now. He's the whole Confederacy. And he made me captain. You heard him say it. Captain Israel Domingo."

"I see," Brandon said. There was nothing more to say. He, too, had long known that for each debt there must be a repayment, and that for each man there was a different measuring stick to gauge how the payment should be made. He remembered Texas then, and again saw that raw and dusty street where the courthouse squatted with the sentry before it. He thought of Buck Elliot and the cornfield and the whispered plotting and what had come of it. He banished these remembrances and let the night enfold him.

The trail was invisible to Brandon, but Domingo moved unerringly; sometimes, when they were again into timber, he warned Brandon in a soft voice of low branches or unexpected turns. After a while Brandon thought he saw a light wink in the distance, but it vanished; and though Brandon strained his eyes, he saw only the trunks of trees, a dense palisade flanking the trail. Then he saw the light again, but once more it vanished. He was sure he smelled wood smoke. He kept looking for the light.

They had been climbing for nearly an hour; they had moved away from the creek, but Brandon again heard its mindless muttering and judged that they had cut across an elbow of land. Soon Domingo held up a warning hand and drew rein, and they sat their saddles on the edge of a little clearing. Before them stood a cabin, its open door showing a yellow rectangle of light.

"There," Domingo said.

Brandon made out the faint shape of horses in a corral beside the cabin; and as he leaned forward in his saddle, a mingling of voices came to him. He asked, "What is this place?"

"Hashknife line shack. They a ranch on the west slope. Ain't no roof but this for a long ways."

"I'm going in," Brandon said and stepped down from his horse.

Saddle leather made its small complaint as Domingo dismounted, too. He stood silently by Brandon; he

looked across the clearing to the cabin. He said then,
"Only four horses."

Brandon, peering hard, hadn't been sure, but he ac-
cepted Domingo's judgment and thought again of the
black panther and all the furry breed that saw in the
dark. Four horses. It took no real arithmetic to tell him
there should be more mounts than that. Halliday had
reported seven or eight in the crew that had taken the
payroll and Gail away from him. Brandon wondered if
Domingo had made a wrong guess in coming here.
Maybe those voices belonged to Hashknife cowhands
spending a night at the line shack. Then he heard Gail.
A fragment of talk came to him above the clatter of the
creek, and he was sure.

He said, "They've sent the others to Salish to get a
message to Sam Whitcomb. He's the girl's father. All the
better for us. Come morning, there'd be twice the outfit
to go up against."

"Good *cunjer*," Domingo said, and his teeth flashed
in a wide and savage smile.

10

PURSUIT AND DISASTER

Brandon had marked a second fall of light from the
cabin and so knew that a window stood in the west wall,
around the corner from the door. He built his strategy
on this knowledge. "I'll take the door," he said. "You get
to the window and cover me. Don't make a play unless
you need to. This is my party."

He felt Domingo move away from him; and he
drifted, too, cruising across the clearing in such a way as
to avoid the fall of light from the open doorway. He was
alert for a posted guard, but none challenged him, yet

the very absence of a guard laid its small warning along
his spine. *They're certain sure of themselves*, he
thought. Maybe they considered the night their protection. And time. He knew now they hadn't sighted him
from any promontory. They must have made allowance
for how long it would take Halliday to reach either the
camp or town and organize pursuit, and thus they were
sure a barricade of miles and hours lay between them
and danger. Yet he did not allow himself to be completely satisfied with this surmise; he held to alertness.

He reached the doorway and stood just beyond the
path of light. By leaning slightly, he had his look inside
and got a partial glimpse of the single room. He could
see one end of a table at which Champ McCoy sat, his
broad back to the door. On that table stood a black
leather bag which Brandon at once recognized, for it
had carried the pay on a score of jobs. On a bench along
the wall, Gail Whitcomb crouched; she wore a tailored
riding outfit, and her hair had come loose so that it
tumbled long and golden on her shoulders. Anger and
defiance showed on her; she looked drawn from long
tension. Sherm Lucas sat beside her, his dark face petulant; he had the look of one whose special pride had
been touched.

Lucas reached now and put his hand on Gail's arm.
She drew away from him. Lucas smiled sourly. McCoy
threw back his big head and laughed. "You're just plain
poison to her, Sherm," he said. "Hours, now, you've
been trying and you haven't caught on yet. Sooner or
later all you lady-killers run up against one who wants
no part of you."

Lucas flung McCoy a forced smile. "She's so used to
Eastern broadcloth, Champ, she doesn't know what a
real man is like." He reached again for Gail and was
rough about it; he pulled her around so that she faced
him. "Isn't it so, honey?"

She showed real fear then, but anger was still in her. She got at Lucas's shin with the toe of her boot, a hard kick. His face twisted with pain, and he let her go. At once she was on her feet and darting toward the door, but Lucas moved as fast. He got his arms around her waist and pulled her back and swung her around so that she faced him. She began beating against his chest, but he made this impossible by hauling her hard against him. He was now a man who had to triumph or lose face; this was plain in his eyes.

He said hoarsely, "There's other ways than arguing with them, Champ."

McCoy said, "None of that, Sherm. The deal didn't include rough stuff. We've still got a dicker to make with Sam Whitcomb, remember."

Pure wickedness bold on him, Lucas said in a breathless voice, "Hell, who's to know? You don't think she's going to tell it far and wide afterward."

Brandon chose then to step through the doorway, his gun in his hand. Whatever showed on his face made Lucas release Gail. She darted aside. In the light of a lantern suspended from the ceiling, Lucas's eyes turned milky. Brandon saw that the cabin held a bunk and a stove in addition to the table he had partially glimpsed. Beside the stove sat two men who were turned motionless as statues by his entrance. McCoy swung around in his chair and almost tilted it over; he let out a huge roar. Gail ran to Brandon's side. Brandon said in a voice he failed to recognize as his own, "I ought to blast the living hell out of every one of you!"

McCoy recovered first. He had half his face turned toward Brandon, and if McCoy sometimes looked like a brutal cherub, he now looked like a sly one. "Brandon, boy, it's a start you've given us. Alone?"

"Of course not," Brandon said and found that he was shaking with anger. He looked at Lucas; Lucas stood with his hands half raised and his shoulders hunched. Brandon said savagely, "Go ahead and try for that gun you're wearing."

Lucas shook his head. "Another day, bucko."

Brandon spoke to Gail without moving his eyes from Lucas. "Cross behind me and pick up that valise. Good! Is it full? Now fade out. You'll find horses at the edge of the clearing. Climb onto the piebald." She had got the valise and come behind him again; he felt her move away from him. He hadn't dared look toward the window before, but now he did and saw that it was open. "Captain," he called. "Come in here and lift their guns. I'm taking the crowd in to Salish."

He hadn't intended to do this. He had come here with no other thought but to recover the payroll and get Gail free and away. The new plan grew out of anger. He wanted Lucas to make a play; and because he knew Lucas wouldn't run the risk, he wanted the man in the Salish calaboose along with these others. He saw that his proposal came as a surprise to them and so hit them hard; they had thought he would settle for less.

Only McCoy remained unruffled. He sat sideways on his chair; he unleashed the charm of his smile and said cajolingly, "Now, Brandon, be a sensible man." Then, suddenly, McCoy upset the chair by leaning his weight against the back of it, and he dived for Brandon's legs as he went down.

Brandon, leaping aside, felt McCoy's weight strike him. He also saw Lucas's hands fall; he knew that Lucas was seizing all the worth there might be in this moment. The two by the stove stirred to life, but sound filled the cabin, and darkness, as the lantern blotted out. Domingo had fired through the window. In the darkness, gun flame sprang at Brandon. That was Lucas shooting. Brandon fired three times, shooting blindly and moving his gun so that it raked the room. In each gun flash he caught movement, vague and meaningless. Something heavy crashed across the table, and a man screamed, his voice high and stricken.

Brandon slammed through the open door. He ran halfway across the clearing, then turned and fired at the dark blob of the doorway. He heard Gail call, "Over here!" her voice clear and high-pitched but not holding panic. Something gigantic shaped up in the night; Brandon tilted his gun, then recognized Domingo. Brandon ran on and got to the piebald. Gail was mounted; Brandon pulled himself up behind her. Domingo caught up reins and heaved himself into his saddle. Domingo said, "Follow me," in a carrying voice.

Gun flame showed redly from the cabin, and Brandon made out vague figures in the clearing. He felt the piebald crash against underbrush and for a moment thought the mare stricken. They hit the creek and splashed into it. Brandon reached around Gail and took the reins. He strained his eyes and saw the great bulk of Domingo just ahead of them.

They got across the creek and into timber. Through this, Domingo found a snaky way. Brandon was completely lost in a closed-in world, but he knew they were dropping downhill. Sometimes they followed ridges; sometimes they came along the looping switchbacks of a crazy trail. After a long while they drew rein in one of those mountain meadows. It might have been the one where Domingo had first come upon him; Brandon couldn't be sure. A creek brawled nearby, but most creeks had the same voice in the night.

Domingo dismounted, and as he'd done on the night of their first meeting, he lowered himself to the ground and put an ear to the earth, listening. He stood up and nodded. "They riding," he announced. "But far away."

Brandon said bitterly, "My first notion was to get Gail, then scatter their horses so they couldn't follow. My second notion was to drag the bunch to jail. Neither worked worth a damn."

Gail asked, "How did you get on the trail?"

"I met Halliday."

"Poor Kirk! He tried to put up a fight. I hope they didn't hurt him badly."

Faint irritation touched Brandon. "He'll live," he said. "Give him a couple days rest, and he'll be able to read the financial news as well as ever."

"You don't like him," she said, her voice showing a real interest in this. "Why is that?"

"He's your man," Brandon said. "Do you have to ask another man what he's like? I have nothing against him. He did the best he could today."

She turned her head so that her profile showed. She was pretty by starlight, and grave. She said, "I'm grateful to you, Holt. I haven't liked thinking of how I treated you the night you came to Dad's car. I want you to know I was never so glad to see anybody in my life as I was to see you tonight."

He had to grin. "You wanted a taste of the woolly life, girl. You got a fair sampling. By the way, did they take any of the payroll money from the valise?"

"Not that I saw." Her voice sounded mildly amused. "Is that the most important thing?"

"Important enough," he said.

Domingo said, "We ride."

Gail asked, "Who is this friend of yours?"

Brandon said, "I'm sorry. Gail, this is Captain Domingo. It was Domingo, really, who got you free of that cabin."

Domingo said again, "We ride," and climbed aboard his horse.

They moved through the night, but not at such a pell-mell pace. They dropped on downward, feeling their way, Domingo always in the lead. The stars told Brandon that midnight was long past; the woods held only the normal night sounds; wherever the pursuit rode, it must be far off. He grew tired, and he felt Gail's weight in his arms and judged that she must be near exhaustion. He wondered if they hadn't better stop and spread the saddle blankets, but Domingo gave no indication of such an intent, and Brandon was trusting Domingo's judgment above his own. He wondered what strange jungle-bred knowledge was this black man's and whether the pursuit was nearer than he, Brandon, supposed.

In dawn's grayness they came to another mountain meadow and here Domingo said, "We rest." Gail slipped to the ground and seated herself on a rock. Her face was gray with strain. Domingo made no move to unsaddle. He seated himself, too, and was like a black idol, his face empty. Brandon, shy on sleep for three nights now, began nodding. He willed wakefulness. He looked at Gail, his interest sharp in spite of himself. He saw her tonight as a maturer woman than he had thought her to be, and he judged her to be a stubborn one.

He asked abruptly, "Why Halliday?"

"How's that?"

"You were shed of him once, and that pleased Sam. Now you've taken up with him again. To spite Sam, I suppose. Are you putting your teeth in one bit to escape another?"

She was at once alert and defensive; he saw the quick rise of her chin. "Maybe I love Kirk."

He shook his head. "Then you'd have to love his way of life. No daughter of Sam Whitcomb's would want anything as certain sure as the years with Kirk Halliday would be. Whatever joy you have would die out. Isn't it so?"

She said with spirit, "So you work for Sam Whitcomb every minute of every day and night!"

He shook his head again. Then he shrugged. "It's no business of mine."

Domingo stood up and lifted himself to the saddle. "Better ride," he said.

"Sure," Brandon said and arose. He felt stiff-muscled and weary, and he had a sense of defeat. He had swayed Gail not at all. He offered his hand to her. "Come on."

The first sunlight found them in the foothills, the timber gone and the land undulating so that they got no real glimpse of what lay ahead or behind. But Domingo had turned as alert as any animal; once again he dismounted and laid an ear to the ground. He looked up and said, "They come."

"Close?" Brandon asked.

"Mighty close."

"Can you tell how many?"

"Three, I think," Domingo said, and Brandon remembered the one who'd screamed in the darkness and crashed across the table.

Domingo mounted again, and Brandon expected to see the black send his horse galloping. But Domingo only urged the horse to a trot. Brandon did likewise; the piebald, double-burdened, had begun to flag. Domingo pulled his own mount down to a walk. They came atop a ridge, and before them spread a great sweep of land, golden in the first light. In the far distance Brandon saw the telegraph line, but he also saw a small knot of horsemen who swept toward them. Four, he judged. Then he understood. Those four who hadn't been at the cabin last night—the ones he'd guessed had ridden to Salish to carry McCoy's terms of ransom to Sam Whitcomb. And now they were riding back.

He looked at Domingo. No reading that black face, but certainly surprise wasn't showing. Now Brandon understood why Domingo had pushed on through the night, yet spared the horses as much as he could, saving their strength for the race that might have to be run. Domingo had gambled that they might escape just such a trap as they now found themselves in.

Brandon looked behind. No sign yet of Lucas and McCoy and that other man who'd survived the cabin fight. No warning drumbeat of hoofs. But Domingo had heard them. They were coming—they were coming. He looked around him. Coulees here and there.

Domingo stepped down from his saddle and dragged the Winchester from its scabbard. He motioned violently to Brandon. "Climb on my horse, suh." He pointed to the left where one of the coulees cut the earth. "Down there."

Brandon shook his head. "She can go ahead. I'll stay with you."

Domingo said, "No need." He pointed across the sweep of grass. "Look!"

Brandon stared, and for the first time saw the great body of riders sweeping down out of the northeast. They were a mile or so from the four horsemen coming from Salish, and it looked as though neither group had yet seen the other. The distance was too great for him to identify any of the larger force, but the direction from which they came told him all he needed to know. He said, with a shake of his head, "Every last man they could round up from camp, and more besides," and he was thinking that Champ McCoy had tallied again.

Domingo said, "Take Miss Gail into the coulee. Stay with her." He cradled the Winchester against his cheek and fired at the four. The distance was too great. He levered the rifle and waited, then fired again. Six-shooters sent up tiny puffs of smoke from the little group, but one among them had a rifle. The first shot gouged up dirt fifty feet ahead of where Brandon stood.

Brandon looked for shelter, but there was only one rock nearby. Domingo had dropped behind it and was resting the Winchester across the top. He waved a huge black hand at Brandon, and Brandon stepped up to the saddle of Domingo's horse.

"Come on!" he shouted and swatted at the piebald's rump with his sombrero as he reined past. The piebald leaped forward. Riding stirrup to stirrup with Gail, Brandon galloped into the coulee. He now saw Domingo's strategy and thus was willing to play the game Domingo's way. It was Gail whom Domingo wanted protected; and while Brandon was seeing to that, Domingo would be keeping those four busy until the crew from camp, alerted by the gunfire, cut them off.

Then Brandon remembered the three who were coming from behind.

He swung his horse around. He heard the cough of Domingo's Winchester. Then the Winchester went silent, but Domingo raised a yell of triumph. Brandon shouted at Gail, "Go on!" and turned the Boxed T mount around and rode back out of the coulee. He saw Domingo running toward another coulee; as he looked, the giant black bobbed out of sight. Those four riders from town had turned tail and were streaking off into the distance. The riders from camp, much closer now, had split into two bunches. The smaller of these had gone racing at an angle to give chase to the four. The rest were coming on.

Brandon swung the borrowed horse back into the coulee, and was astonished to find Gail awaiting him. "Straight ahead," Brandon shouted. The coulee became wide enough to let them again run side by side; they followed a small creek that had cut this ravine through the ages. They could glimpse only the brushy walls and the sky overhead. The coulee twisted and turned and seemed almost to double back on itself.

Half a mile along, they came around a bend and saw before them nearly a score of horsemen. Sam Whitcomb was at their head; his face looked a thousand years old till he sighted Gail. Kirk Halliday, big and awkward in a saddle, rode with the group. Jake Fargo was here, too, and Brandon recognized post-hole diggers and wire stringers and the teamster.

Gail flung herself off the piebald and made a lurching run toward Whitcomb. Dismounting, Whitcomb caught her and held her close till Halliday got down and came and took Gail from him. Jake Fargo's whiskery face was bland, but he winked at Brandon.

Brandon, slipping from the Boxed T horse, said, "Seems you fetched everybody but the cook."

Whitcomb had the look of one who'd walked a long mile with terror and hopelessness. He said, "It took half the night to raise enough saddle horses. But we were ready to comb the hills fine."

Brandon said, "There's a big black man around somewhere. For God's sake, don't any of you line sights on him. He's a friend."

Whitcomb said, "I think the shooting's all over." Then his face turned startled. He gazed upward at the brushy wall of the coulee, and Brandon heard the explosion of a six-shooter and realized Whitcomb was hit and going down. He reached forward and caught Whitcomb's rangy body and lowered him to the ground. He saw the pain on Whitcomb's face; he saw the blood on the man's shoulder. The coulee had become a milling chaos of horses and men. Some of the telegraph crew had guns out; their guns and Brandon's spoke, and lead clipped the leaves from bushes high above, but there was no target. Only the echo of a laugh drifted back. Brandon knew that laugh.

For the second time he'd forgotten the three who were coming from behind. But it was Champ McCoy who'd laughed and tallied once more. Down on one knee, Brandon searched the coulee's rim, then slowly put his gun away.

11

THE WAYS OF WOMEN

They got Whitcomb to Salish in the afternoon and put him to bed in the Ballard House, and here Jonathan King dug the lead from Sam's shoulder and dressed the wound. Whitcomb was running a slight temperature. King had cleared the room of everyone but Brandon, even shooing Gail away.

Brandon stood by the window and looked at Whitcomb's lined face with its thin film of sweat. This room depressed Brandon. It might have been the very one in which he'd slept, only the calendar was different; he felt closed-in and like a traveler who'd finished out a futile circle. He made a tired gesture with his hands.

"It adds up to a poor day," he said, and he was remembering that Lucas and McCoy and that third man had got clear away. "Those two that the boys rounded up are now sitting in the calaboose, Sam. But I can't begin to figure the work that we lost."

Whitcomb said, "Gail's safe."

"And the payroll," Brandon said. "But we'll have to work night shifts to catch up."

"We've got more men coming," Whitcomb reminded him. "I'll shunt them out to camp as fast as they show."

"Green hands," Brandon said disgustedly.

"We'll break them in, Holt."

King, busily stowing instruments in his black case, looked up. His face showed disapproval. "You'll stay in bed a couple of weeks, Mr. Whitcomb. That's an order.

Brandon, you see that he obeys it. He can run a tele-graph line if he likes, but he'll have to do his managing from bed."

"Better hog-tie him," Brandon said.

King departed. Brandon made a move toward the door, too. In him was an impatience to be back on the job, and there was nothing more he could do for Sam. The smell of antiseptics hung heavy here, and pain was a gray presence, too.

Whitcomb turned his glazed face toward Brandon and made a weak gesture. "I've got to load the whole thing on your shoulders, Holt. Till I can get out of bed."

"I know," Brandon said. "I'll make out."

"But the job includes Gail now."

"Oh, hell," Brandon said.

Whitcomb moved himself against the pillow so as to favor that wounded shoulder. "She's engaged to Halli-day again. Funny, I haven't got a thing against him but a feeling I can't name, Holt. Just the same, I don't believe her happiness lies with him. If you can manage to keep her from doing something she'll be sorry for, I'll be grateful."

"Give her your blessing," Brandon said. "Tell her you think Kirk's just fine and you hope they'll get married this evening, if not sooner. I'll bet she'll decide that she isn't half as interested in him as she thought she was. You've tried to keep a hobble on her, Sam. It's the worst thing you could do."

Whitcomb gave him a quick, shrewd appraisal. "So you've talked to her, eh?"

"Some."

Whitcomb shook his head. "It goes deeper than you think. You see, I'd picked a man for her and told her so. Long ago. That was a mistake. I guess it's stubbornness that drives her to Halliday. She wouldn't be fooled if I changed suddenly."

Brandon shrugged. "I'll do what I can. But I can't be out at camp and here, too."

"She'll be sticking close to my bedside as long as I'm in bad shape, Holt. If she starts getting notional about Kirk, I'll know it. And I'll get word to you."

Brandon again moved toward the door. He stood before it and had a last look over his shoulder at Whitcomb. A crippled longhorn. An old mossy-horn bogged down and pestered by yapping coyotes and small flies till he'd grown almost too tired to bellow. A fighter with a last bit of fight left in him. Brandon remembered what he owed this man, and he said in a soft voice, "Don't let a thing worry you. Just call if you need me."

"I'll do that, Holt. Don't work yourself to death. If we fail on this contract, we'll find another somewhere."

"Sure," Brandon said. But he was thinking: *He's whistling in the dark.*

On the street, he found Salish a sour town by daylight, numbed and spiritless after its excesses of the night. A sick town. The false fronts looked harsh and naked and weathered in the sun; the street lay littered with the sweepings of the saloons; and such people as moved about seemed heavy-footed and disinterested in their own doings. He remembered Jonathan King's hopes for this town and shook his head.

He got Domingo's big horse from the hitchrail before the Ballard House and led it along. There'd been no more trace of Domingo after that coulee fracas than there'd been of Lucas and McCoy. Brandon himself had made the hunt. Two prisoners bagged, though, from the four who'd been coming from town. A pair of two-bit badmen not worth the keep the county would now bestow upon them.

Brandon had let Gail ride the piebald to town, but he now intended to pick up the mare for the return journey to camp. He walked along the street, leading the

Boxed T horse; he remembered the slow and weary ride from the foothills, with Whitcomb reeling in a saddle but not wanting to wait for a wagon to be fetched.

He saw two of his own crew before one of the saloons; these two had been part of the group that had ridden in with Whitcomb as a bodyguard of sorts. The bulk of the outfit had gone back to camp, with Jake Fargo leading them. Damn it, Jake had a wounded shoulder, too, and shouldn't have been cavorting around on a saddle horse. He'd likely be stove up for a week. Brandon looked at the pair on the saloon steps in an unsmiling manner. "You've got your pay in your pants," he said. "I don't want you showing up tomorrow with heads you couldn't get through a barn door. Round up the others and start back to camp."

He didn't wait to see how they took this, but he felt their scowls follow him. He walked along until he reached Mountain's headquarters and saw the piebald tied before the place. Through the window, he thought he made out the bulk of Kirk Halliday. He remembered that he'd asked Halliday to have Jake Fargo keep the crew working yesterday. But he couldn't blame Halliday, or Jake, either, for following an order from Sam Whitcomb.

He'd got the Boxed T horse ready for leading and had moved himself from one saddle to the other when Gail appeared in the office doorway. Her face showed an immediate interest and a deep flow of feeling, and it held sadness, too. She asked, "How's Dad?"

"He'll have to keep to bed for a couple of weeks," he said more gruffly than he'd intended.

This slight show of antagonism must have reached through to her, for her chin came up. "Could it be," she asked, "that you hold me responsible for Dad's stopping a bullet?"

He shrugged. "If you'd stayed in town in the first

place, you wouldn't have got carried off. And he wouldn't have had to come hunting you."

She was beautiful in the doorway; she was proud and contrite and angry. He could see the successive waves of her feelings break over her, and he watched to see which one would sweep her the furthest. At last she said, "What you say is true. I'm properly sorry, and I judge that I've been spanked. What can I do, Holt?"

"You can visit him every day and sit for a while. He'd like that."

She nodded. "And I would like that, too." She smiled, and he saw in that smile an effort to reach out to him. "I'm grateful to you, Holt. More grateful than I know how to say."

"Thank Domingo," he said and turned away from the hitchrail and led the Boxed T horse along the street.

At once the big cayuse moved up and bit at the rump of the piebald. Brandon took the slack out of the lead rope. Passing a livery stable, he had a notion to leave the borrowed mount there but decided against this. The camp was nearer to Boxed T, and Domingo would come for the horse. Perhaps Colonel Templeton would come, also, fetching the crew of the valley ranch. That menace still hung over Mountain Telegraph, like the clouds about the peaks that threatened rain and waited the moment.

String wire, and you lose yourself in the endless race, not knowing one day from another but realizing that each day is a leaf fallen from the calendar, each day brings the deadline nearer; and always the poles set between suns seem not enough. The ground is stubborn and repels the pick and the shovel, a batch of insulators proves inferior and has to be returned to Salish, and three of your crew slip away to see the lights of town and buck the tiger and fill a painted woman's shoe with silver. Poles are late in arriving, and the crew sent to fetch them reports a brush with hidden marksmen who keep them busy with guns when they should have been using axes. The wire stringers stand idle that day. The long lightning is flung from camp to town, shouting always for more supplies, more men; and you hammer the key constantly and wish that Sam Whitcomb were up and about and doing the job at the other end.

Thus Brandon spent his time. Again the work went on from dawn to dusk, and again the brush fires burned when the crew worked overtime. The first of the new help arrived soon after his return from Salish, brought in fast by the new railroad spur and shunted by wagon to the Valley of the Three Sisters. Green men, most of them, but some were old hands who had worked for the myriad independent outfits that had flourished a score of years before. Jake Fargo, stiff in the shoulder but otherwise a sound man, broke in the untrained ones and swapped tall tales by firelight with the old hands.

Halliday rode out to camp one day to discuss some problems of supply. Gail wasn't with him, as Brandon was quick to note. Halliday took the buggy back to Salish, tying his saddle horse behind it. The buggy had been here at camp since the day Gail had been kidnapped.

The crew was nothing to kick about, save for the green hands. Spreading the payroll money around had helped, as Brandon soon admitted. Some, like the three who'd slipped away, had got restless from having money in their pockets, but most were saving their pay for Warlock. Spirits were higher, and there was no more whispering that Mountain Telegraph was broke and so unable to pay off. But still Brandon had to lash the men on, for the sands were running out. In more ways than one, Brandon reflected. With another week behind him, he was that much nearer to Boxed T, and Templeton hadn't yet showed back.

What was it the man had said? "I shall return within the week." Let's see, that had been a couple of days before Gail had been kidnapped and the payroll lifted. Well over a week now. What a heap had happened since then! Brandon remembered that ride through the heart of night and his witnessing the moonlit meeting between Lucas and Ellen Templeton. He could still feel the hot blood rise whenever he thought of Lucas, for there was also that raid on the camp to remember, and that night when he and Domingo had closed in on Hashknife's line cabin. Domingo hadn't showed, and the Boxed T cayuse grew fat on valley grass and lazy from no load to pack.

On a morning, Brandon called Jake Fargo to his tent. "Take over today, Jake," Brandon said. "I'm going for a ride."

"Town?"

"No, I'm going to return that horse to Boxed T."

Fargo gave him a sidelong glance that held a shadow of dismay. "Any point in stirring up a hive when the bees ain't buzzing?"

"Maybe not," Brandon said. "Just the same, I'm going."

"Suit yourself," Fargo said.

Brandon set out shortly, again riding the piebald and leading the borrowed horse. He knew, as Jake had known, that the horse was only an excuse; he had to know the situation at Boxed T, and this was a way to learn it. Better knowing than endlessly waiting for an attack that didn't come. It was a wise man who'd first observed that anticipation was worse than trouble. There was a hope, too—the hope that he'd swayed Ellen Templeton to his way of thinking that night on the rim above Boxed T. Maybe she'd since been able to persuade her father to a different view. Slim chance, considering the peculiar madness of Templeton; but still the hope persisted.

Not so far to Boxed T as it had been, not with the telegraph camp pushing nearer. He came across the flat country he'd once ridden by night; he rode in the bold sunlight that glittered from the metal trim of his bridle and forced him to keep his sombrero brim tugged low. Summer flowers were showing now, wild roses and silken sunflowers, and he remembered that girl in the Salish restaurant who'd awaited the flowers so breathlessly. Damned pretty sight at that. He hadn't been looking much farther than the farthest post hole lately, but now the flowers were all around him and hit the eye. He wondered if a man like Halliday noticed the flowers and picked a few each day for Gail. It was somehow a sour thought.

Soon he came to the rougher country where the wind-twisted junipers stood in their eternal writhings. Tortured-looking trees, reminding him of Sam Whitcomb when Champ McCoy's bullet had struck the man. He was thinking about this when he reached the place where the land dropped away and the buildings of Boxed T sprawled below.

He picked an easy place and began the descent. He rode slowly, trying to look like a man come on peaceful business and so easy in his mind, but he felt a tightness in his belly as he drew closer to the long, low main building. A porch ran the width of the house. You saw mighty few porches on Montana ranch houses, but Boxed T had one. Alan Templeton sat in a rocker on the porch. Behind him was a window, and to his left a door. These things Brandon marked at once, needing a close knowledge of the surroundings if there should be trouble. Templeton had a Winchester rifle leaning against the porch railing. He stood up as Brandon brought the horses closer. He picked up the Winchester and held it loosely under one arm.

Brandon made sure that his hands were in plain sight. He nudged back his sombrero. "Good afternoon," he said. "I've come to return a horse."

Templeton nodded. He was wearing ranch garb today, but his manner was as military as though the uniform clothed him. He showed neither friendliness nor animosity; his voice held a grave, impersonal courtesy. "Domingo's mount, sir. He told me he'd loaned the mount to a friend who would surely return it soon. May I ask how you came by it?"

"I'm the friend," Brandon said.

Templeton's lean face clouded, and he shifted the rifle slightly. Around them the ranch yard droned; Brandon had seen nobody at the corrals or near the bunkhouse, and thus he could count on no one to step between him and this man's madness. He thought that something stirred behind the window at Templeton's back, but he couldn't be sure. He kept his eyes on Templeton and schooled his face to stillness.

Templeton said, "What kind of ruse is this, man?"

Brandon shrugged. "Do you want the horse, or do I take it back?"

"Just leave the mount. One of my men will put him in the corral."

"Sure," Brandon said. "That's all I wanted. You've got your horse, and I'll be going."

Templeton relaxed a little. He looked like a man torn between an habitual courtesy and a present wariness. He said, "I'm sorry not to be able to offer you hospitality and refreshments after your ride. You realize my position. At best, we're under an armed truce."

This was like walking a dangerous street where some doorways were safe and some not. Yet Brandon now chose to be forthright. "Yes," he said. "I expected you back at my camp before this."

Templeton nodded. "My daughter and Captain Domingo and my physician have all tried to persuade me that I am in error about the nature of your enterprise, sir. I remain unconvinced. I have written a full report to General Longstreet and am awaiting his orders."

Don't laugh! Brandon thought. General Longstreet! He couldn't have sworn whether the man was alive or dead. Last time he'd heard, Longstreet had been appointed minister to Turkey. But that had been quite a while back, while Grant was President. It had struck Brandon at the time that it was mighty kind of a Yankee to pass out a fat job to a Reb, but maybe Grant had held a fighting man's respect for Longstreet.

"You'll wait for an answer?" Brandon asked.

"Not long," Templeton said. "Perhaps the general is busy. Perhaps he is wounded. The fortunes of war, you know. Shortly I shall have to act without his instructions."

Brandon lifted his reins. He'd learned what he'd come to learn, and he had no argument to give Templeton. Ellen had tried and so had Domingo and Doc King, and his persuasiveness would be no greater than theirs. He was the enemy, because the years were all tangled in Alan Templeton's mind. No changing that. He felt sorry for Templeton and warm toward the man; Templeton reminded him a bit of Judge Elliot down in Texas who'd gone on fighting a war that was over and had been jailed by the damyanks for his trouble.

Brandon only said now, "I hope the general will persuade you that you're wrong, Colonel."

He'd wheeled his horse about and was fifty yards from the porch when Ellen called to him. "Holt! Wait a moment!" He neck-reined the mount and saw her come running across the yard toward him. She looked free and wild, and the sight of her stirred him. She was wearing a holstered forty-five as she had that night with Lucas, and this surprised him. She reached his stirrup and stood breathless, her cheeks red and her breasts heaving. She said, "You couldn't budge him?"

He shook his head. He looked back toward the porch and saw that Templeton was seated again and showing no great interest in them. Templeton now looked like a tired old man taking his ease, and all Boxed T held an air of peace and timelessness. Brandon said, "No, Ellen. He's still got his mind set."

"Domingo told me about your night in the hills and how he came to turn his horse over to you," she said. "He figured that you'd return the horse. We both hoped my father would take that as a friendly act."

The big cayuse was now ambling around a corner of the ranch house toward the corral gate. Brandon watched it go. "You'll have to tell Domingo his scheme didn't work," he said. He smiled at Ellen. He had never seen her before in daylight, but he was pleased with what he saw. He shared a secret with her and felt drawn close to her because of that; the secret no longer seemed tinged with shame. He remembered how she had looked by moonlight on the rim above; he remembered how troubled she'd been and how forthright. He said, "I hope all is well with you."

She said, "You mean Sherm, don't you?"

He nodded, at once knowing the faint clamor of the anger that had been his at Hashknife's line cabin. "Did Domingo tell you everything that happened?"

"Yes," she said, and her lips drew tight. "He told me. Last night the lantern waved. I took your advice. I tried putting it out with a rifle. I missed, I'm sure, but he didn't linger."

He saw now that she had forsaken the last of a dubious ideal, and he could guess what this had cost her. You fashioned someone to your mind's fancy and that phantom became real enough to die hard. "What next?" he asked.

"He'll come for that iron box," she said. "Now he knows the other way will never work."

He shook his head. He could understand why she was wearing a gun, and the irony was that Lucas was his enemy and Boxed T's, too; yet there could be no truce with Templeton. It was all as mixed up as a sackful of snakes. But he kept his smile showing for Ellen.

"Don't worry," he said. "He'll not be that bold." But he didn't believe this himself, and her face told him that she didn't, either. He lifted his hand and let it fall and brought the horse around. She had turned back toward the house when he took the trail to the top of the rim.

12

SMASH THE MAN DOWN!

By firelight, Jake Fargo, having been patient beyond endurance, asked, "How were things at the beehive?"

Brandon, back several hours, put his supper plate in the wrecking pan. "He's written to General Longstreet for orders." He saw Fargo's whiskery face pucker; then Jake thought better of laughing and merely shook his head. Brandon said, "He's not going to wait for an answer, though. Not much longer. Better issue guns all around, Jake, and see that the men keep them handy." He yawned and stretched. "Me for my tent. The days are mighty long, you notice."

Thus Mountain's crew came to carry pistols strapped at their waists, and rifles stood stacked and ready. Brandon assigned men to stand guard by day as well as by night. Green hands who couldn't tell an insulator from a piece of Indian fooforaw could shoulder a rifle and so make themselves useful. To Brandon the question was not whether Templeton would come, but *when;* and there was still the menace of Sherm Lucas and Champ McCoy and the remnants of their outlaw riders. Two in jail now, and one dead in the hills, but Lucas might have recruited more.

Not enough force to attack the enlarged crew, apparently. But hidden marksmen could harass the pole cutters; and the day after Brandon's visit to Boxed T, a freighter was stopped on his way from Salish and his wagon was overturned and burned. Lucas again. The wire was cut and left dangling, but the break was soon located and repaired. Brandon then debated whether to put men patrolling the line. He decided he couldn't spare his crew for such work. You'd spread yourself too thin if you took to watching every rat hole.

The next morning he got a message summoning him to Salish. The wire had been dictated by Sam Whitcomb and sent by one of the town operators. Certainly it was not Halliday's inept hand at the key. M-U-S-T S-E-E Y-O-U A-T O-N-C-E, Whitcomb said; and Brandon hit the saddle for Salish.

He rode with a sharp remembrance that once he'd been ambushed on this trail. All things had come to be shaded with suspicion in his mind. That message might have been faked through some devious doing of Champ McCoy, yet no one blocked the way for Brandon as they had that day he'd taken to the rocks and held off Lucas's crew. A lot more miles from camp to town than there'd been at that time. A man could wring some satisfaction from such an observation.

He reached Salish in midafternoon and went directly to the Ballard House. In the hotel hallway he found a bored-looking man seated on a tilted-back chair. He recognized the fellow as one of Mountain's town employees and was recognized in turn. The man had a gun, not holstered but held in his lap. Brandon grinned. Sam Whitcomb, remembering that raid on his private car, was playing safe.

He found Whitcomb seated in a chair by the window of his room. Ten days now since Sam had been wounded. He looked thinner, but he was perky enough, considering that he'd had a rough session.

"King know you're out of bed?" Brandon asked.

"I whittled him down, Holt."

"You wanted to see me, Sam?"

"It's Gail," Whitcomb said.

He was a man burdened by a load beyond his bearing, and it showed on him when Brandon looked closer. New lines in the face, and the generous mouth was drawn tight at the corners. Hark up in your mind that old Texas town with its dusty street and remember this man standing on that street, seventeen years younger, and you could see what the years had done to Sam Whitcomb. Time laid its own slow ambush, and you couldn't ride around it or fight your way through it; you could only hope that you wouldn't have too many scars to show for the years.

"She hasn't run off with Halliday?" Brandon asked, and felt himself tighten.

Whitcomb shook his head. "Halliday wants her to marry him right away. She's told me so. I asked her to wait until the line reaches Warlock, so I'd be free to stage a proper wedding. She put it up to him. He's too impatient for that. There's a preacher here, but Halliday's not of the man's persuasion, so he wants to drive her to Missoula. From there they'll go East. One of these days they'll light out. It might be today. I get the idea Halliday's determined."

Brandon shaped up a cigarette. "She'd buck your

wish?" The match broke between his fingers and he fished another from his hatband.

Whitcomb grinned. "I should have stayed in bed. She was mighty attentive while I was down. I guess I got too emphatic when this marriage business came along. You gave me good advice when you told me not to hobble her, but I must have forgot to heed it. You see, she comes by her stubbornness honestly."

"Yes," Brandon said, for he knew now that they were indeed alike, father and daughter; and he could see how this had made a constant war between them. Something in the thought brought up a bright picture of Gail as he'd last seen her, proud and contrite and angry, but showing a true concern for Sam Whitcomb. She'd been born of Sam's passion and was therefore a part of Sam, and Brandon felt drawn closer to her by the fullness of this realization. But a faint irritation touched him, too, for at this moment he saw his debt to Whitcomb as something perpetuated and turned endless.

He spurted smoke through his nostrils. "What's to be done about it?"

"Find her and take her to camp with you," Whitcomb urged. "Keep her up there till you reach Warlock. It shouldn't be more than a couple of weeks."

"Camp's no place for her," Brandon said bluntly.

"I know, Holt. But it's the only place where she can be kept safe from him."

"Suppose she won't come?"

"Then you'll have to drag her along," Whitcomb said, his mouth growing tighter. "That's an order, Holt."

Brandon shrugged. "Where will she likely be?"

"She has a room here, three doors down the hall on this same side. If she's not in it, she's probably at headquarters with Halliday. He's been teaching her telegraphy."

Brandon found a cuspidor in the room and dropped his cigarette into it. "I'll wire you from camp," he said.

He went along the hall to the room Whitcomb had mentioned and rapped on the door. No answer. He rapped again and listened for the fall of footsteps. The bored-looking guard said in a bored voice, "She went out about an hour ago."

Brandon said, "You could have told me before I skinned my knuckles raw."

He went down to the street. Somewhere, not too distantly, a locomotive hooted, the sound drifting across space to fall on the town like a sad benediction. The end-of-track must be almost to Salish, Brandon reflected. He stepped up to the piebald's saddle and reined the mare along toward headquarters. He had to see Halliday anyway; there was that matter of the defective insulators that had come through. He wanted Halliday to be sure that a different product was ordered in the future. Those insulators hadn't been any more effective than the mudball kind used back in the 'forties, that had washed off in the first rain! If Whitcomb were on the job, mistakes like that wouldn't be happening.

All these minor nuisances added to the weight on Brandon. He was a sour man, thinking about this, and thinking, too, of the order that had been handed him. *Build me a telegraph line, son. And in your spare time, keep my daughter from making a damned fool of herself. It's all in the day's work, boy.*

He was brought from his moodiness by the sound of his own name. "Hey, Brandon! Hold up!"

It was a remembered voice saying the remembered words, and Brandon was brought around in his saddle. He was abreast of the Hogshead; and Champ McCoy again stood on the porch, a bigness beneath the overhang, his bright smile showing, and his hands thrust deep into his pockets. It might have been that earlier encounter, save that this was daylight. And between now and that night when McCoy had called to him from this same stand, there'd been that affair at Hashknife's line cabin; yes, and that bullet from the coulee's rim that had cut down Sam Whitcomb. The rest you could discount—the raids and the cut wire—for these were of the old, old pattern and so not personal.

Brandon urged the piebald up to the saloon's steps and said flatly, "You're a damn bold one, Champ, to be showing your face in town."

"And why do you say that, my friend?"

"They've got a cell in the jail just your size."

A happy cherub, McCoy, satisfied with himself and with the world. He teetered on his toes in pure joyousness, not drunk as he'd been the other time. "And what would put me in a cell? Your word against mine? Who would listen to that big darky, even if he were here to speak against me and so bolster your story? Or maybe you're thinking that those two you got locked up will testify against me. I think not. 'Tis Consolidated money they'll want backing them when they come to trial. But we're wasting the best part of a bright day. Will you come inside and have a drink? Out of my own pocket I'll pay for it."

Brandon shook his head. "The hell with you, Champ," he said, making this flat and emphatic. He folded his arms and leaned on the saddle horn. "So you weren't in that cabin up in the hills?"

"A million miles away I was. Back at Consolidated's office in the East talking big business to come. Wire and ask them, if you don't think so."

"Suppose I ask Gail Whitcomb instead, Champ. Maybe she'll remember you, too."

McCoy pursed his lips. "A saucy one, that girl. Too bad you broke up the fandango when you did."

The bold effrontery of the man had stirred a certain amusement in Brandon in spite of himself; but his mood swung instantly, a harsh anger taking hold of him. He straightened in his saddle. "Meaning, Champ?"

"Meaning Sherm might have taught her something she didn't learn in any of the fancy schools Sam Whitcomb sent her to," McCoy said. His smile turned brightly evil. "Damned if I wouldn't have liked a hand in that. You'd feel the same, Brandon, if you didn't work for Whitcomb. A man takes his fun where he finds it. Ain't it so?"

Brandon said, "There's been a day marked on the calendar for a long time, Champ. This is the day." Kicking free of the stirrups, he tossed a leg over, and putting his hands to cantle and horn, he launched himself straight at McCoy.

He had time to remember Whitcomb's feeling that this might also be the day when Gail would elope with Halliday. But the thought went through him like a gusty wind, leaving a single moment of coolness before racketing onward. The staying thought was that McCoy had counted him to be of McCoy's own kind. He hit the solidness of the man, but McCoy had got his hands out of his pockets. His arms went around Brandon, and the two of them struck the porch flooring. Locked together, they rolled down the steps and almost under the hoofs of the mare. The piebald snorted and reared and was for a moment a great blackness blotting out the sun.

Breaking free, Brandon got to his feet and saw McCoy lurch to a stand and come at him. No smile on McCoy now. McCoy's fists were a swarm that stung Brandon, beating the breath from him and filling his head with a roar. McCoy's fists seemed everywhere. He closed with McCoy in desperation and got his arms around the man and tried to pull McCoy hard against him, but this was like having hold of an avalanche. Mc-

Coy slipped away from him; Brandon got a grip on McCoy's plaid shirt and brought the man close. The two of them tripped and fell upon the steps and writhed there, each trying to get at the other's throat.

McCoy cursed and managed to smash a fist against Brandon's mouth. Brandon tasted the salt of his own blood and was then a man stripped of all wisdom, holding only to instinct. McCoy tried to get his gun free, but Brandon wrenched the gun from him and flung it aside. McCoy struck at his crotch with a knee, but they were too tightly entwined for this effort to be effective. Brandon got the heel of one hand against McCoy's nose and pushed hard till McCoy, bellowing, broke free.

McCoy hauled himself up. At this very spot he'd once said that he laughed when he fought and that he fought for the fun of it. But he was not laughing, and there was in him no desire but to kill; this desire showed plain. He lowered his head and came butting at Brandon. Brandon straightened him with an uppercut and saw McCoy's arms flail wildly as the man struggled for balance. Brandon came hard after him, knowing he must wring full worth out of this advantage. He smashed his knuckles against the barrel of McCoy's chest; he tried hard for another clean hit at his jaw. McCoy went down into the dust, but he caught at Brandon's belt and dragged him down. Again they rolled over and over, in peril of the piebald's hoofs.

In Brandon there was no thought of his gun, no desire but to smash McCoy. They were up again and standing toe to toe slugging; he saw McCoy's face turn shapeless and become something from a nightmare. He knew that McCoy's fists were getting at him, too, but he was numb to pain. There was nothing in all the wide world but the need to get another clean hit at that jaw. But when he did find McCoy's jaw, he had no real awareness of doing so; and he saw with astonishment that McCoy went down.

McCoy rolled over and pulled himself up till he was on his hands and knees. Brandon stood waiting, his arms wooden and heavy, his fists puffy. McCoy clumsily groped at his empty holster. He shook his head and muttered something that made no sense. He settled very gently down to the earth and rolled over upon his back again and flung his arms out. He sighed gustily, and consciousness went out of him.

Only then did Brandon sense that a ring of men had been drawn by the fight, for their voices had not really penetrated to him. Townsmen and saloon hangers-on, they crowded the porch and some stood in the street; and one had led the piebald a safe distance away. Brandon looked down at McCoy and wondered if he should have that great hulk hauled to jail. He remembered McCoy's surety and Consolidated's power and supposed that McCoy would be out on bail by nightfall. He shook his head, finding it hard to hold to any thought. He took a lurching step in an unsteady world. He tried to fix his eyes on the man who held the piebald. He looked down at McCoy again and said, "Some of you better drag him off the street."

He turned and by an effort of concentration walked to the man who held the mare, and took the reins. That saddle looked higher than a mountain peak, so he chose to lead the piebald. He came along the middle of the street, trying hard to keep his steps steady; he had that kind of pride. He stopped at a horse trough and looked at his reflection in the water and saw that his lips were shapeless and puffy and that the skin was broken on his cheek and over one eye. One of the crowd came up and said, "Here's your hat," and thrust a sombrero at him. He hadn't remembered losing his hat. He nodded.

He washed himself, splashing the water against his

face again and again. He ducked his head in the trough and pushed back his hair with his hands. He felt used-up and not proud of himself. He remembered his thought of many days ago about a man becoming akin to the one he fought.

He walked on to divisional headquarters and tied the piebald at the rack and went inside. The operator on duty was as taciturn as all of his kind, but he showed a startled face and so was more of a mirror than the horse trough had been. The operator was the only person behind the long counter.

"Gail Whitcomb been here this afternoon?" Brandon asked.

"Out back," the operator said.

Brandon went around the end of the counter and through the back door and thus came into the wagon yard. Here, where the empty wagons waited and supplies stood heaped, he had left his mount that night he'd stayed at the Ballard House. And here he saw the familiar buggy that Halliday used for his trips to and from camp. Gail was on the seat of the buggy; Halliday had just handed her up.

Brandon said, "Wait a minute."

Gail looked at him and caught her breath quickly. "Holt! Your face!"

Halliday turned around and gave Brandon a frown. "It sounded like a fight up the street. So you were mixed into it." His manner was that of a man bent upon important business but forced to delay his affairs to acknowledge a triviality.

Brandon asked bluntly, "Are you heading for Missoula?"

Gail said, "So Dad sent you!"

"That doesn't matter," Brandon said. "Climb down."

Halliday at once turned truculent. "Now, see here—" he began, but Brandon was done with talking, having no further patience. He came up to Halliday and put his hand against Halliday's chest and pushed until he had pinned the man against a buggy wheel. Brandon said again to Gail, "Climb down," and saw the fury grow in Halliday's face to become a thing beyond control.

Twice today, Brandon thought, and made ready to fight again.

13

THE TALE IS TOLD

Halliday drew in his breath and let it out in a harsh gust of sound, his red face redder and his shoulders hunched. Brandon watched him closely. He had long since judged Halliday to be an opportunist, an opinionated man with a tendency to arrogance; but he'd never considered Halliday as dangerous. Not till now. Still, he could remember that Halliday had put up a fight of sorts that day Lucas and McCoy had snatched Gail from this very buggy; and there was now another fight in Halliday. The man brought up his fists and came off the buggy wheel. He said hotly, "You've overstepped, Brandon. You've been edging toward insolence for a long time. I've had enough of you."

Here was opportunism again, Brandon knew, for the ravages of McCoy's fists stood plain on him, and Halliday had only to pit himself against the ragged reserve that was left. Brandon had a gun, while Halliday appeared unarmed; but Halliday was counting on that very fact to disarm Brandon. Surety showed on the man. Brandon shoved at Halliday again and sent him back against the wheel. Brandon said flatly, "There's no need to fight. You're just not going to Missoula. Get that through your head!"

Halliday struck at him. Brandon raised his arms and warded off the blow, but his arms were wooden, the movement like something done under water.

He heard Gail cry out, "Kirk! Let him alone!"

This so surprised Brandon that he wanted to risk a look at the girl but didn't dare. Her voice reached through Halliday's fury and turned the man's mouth slack with astonishment. He put his eyes on Brandon; his eyes shone. Then Brandon saw that gaze drop and knew that for the moment Halliday had lost.

Brandon seized this shift in the situation for all it was worth. He had twice ordered Gail from the buggy, but still she sat. In the box behind the buggy seat was one suitcase; on the floor, propped against the dashboard, stood another. Brandon swung up into the buggy, clambered over the suitcase, and with a quick motion unwrapped the reins from around the whipstock. He hauled on the reins and backed the buggy. Halliday stood watching him and then, understanding Brandon's intent, leaped toward the buggy. Halliday's voice lifted; his face was a red flame. But Brandon, cramping the front wheels hard, had got the buggy around, and he shouted at the horse and slapped the reins and went wheeling through the rear gate of the wagon yard at a hard run.

He brought the buggy down the alley and turned a corner crazily and turned another and so came into the main street. He sawed on the reins and pulled the buggy up alongside the boardwalk.

"Which is his suitcase?" he asked.

Gail stared at him, her face puzzled. She nodded toward the suitcase at their feet.

"I'll drop it off at headquarters," he said. "We'll keep yours. You're going to camp with me."

"Dad's orders?" she asked.

He shook his head. "That doesn't matter. The point is that you're going."

She laughed, the sound gay and throaty; on her face was the old impishness he'd seen that night in Sam Whitcomb's private car. She, too, shook her head. She said, "Do you know, you're the only man in the world who would think that such a simple idea would work. Can't you see that the best you can hope is to delay the marriage? I'll steal a horse at camp. Or I'll catch a ride with one of the freighters the first moment your back is turned. Tomorrow, maybe. Or the day after, or the day after that."

He saw one way to delay her, and he didn't take time to explore that way lest he find it studded with obstacles. He knew how willful she could be; he'd been told by Sam Whitcomb, and he'd had his own samples. Now he was pitted against her; it made just one more fight. He had grown weary of fighting. His thinking was fuzzy and desperate and held little deviousness. He asked, "Where's that preacher—the one Halliday didn't favor?"

Her face turned blank with surprise. "What do you want with him?"

"I want to know where he lives. Better tell me. I can ask any man on the street."

She shrugged; her lips showed mild amusement. "The square log house to the left, down at the west end," she said. "Just before you get out of town."

The extra suitcase forgotten, he slapped the horse with the lines and set the buggy rolling again. He trotted the horse along the street to the far fringe of Salish and saw the little log house Gail had indicated. A fence, badly in need of repairs and paint, surrounded the place; the gate sagged open.

He pulled the buggy before the gate and swung to the ground and offered his hand to Gail. "Get down," he said firmly. He saw rebellion in her face; but something else was there, too, some vast puzzlement as to his intentions. She hesitated, then took his hand and let him help her alight.

He got her by the elbow and steered her through the gate and up to the door of the house. She was wearing a traveling suit and a jaunty hat with the veil thrown back; she looked more mature than he had before seen her. He knocked; the door opened, and a plump, gray-haired woman with a friendly, bovine face stood before him. Brandon asked, "Is the preacher home?"

The woman said, "Come in. Come in."

Brandon thrust Gail ahead of him into a little parlor. A man scratched with a pen at an immense desk, a lanky man, bony of face, bony of figure. A man who'd been gaunted down, Brandon judged, by weary miles of circuit-riding and poor eating and the shouldering of the woes of a scattered flock. Brandon asked, "You an ordained preacher?"

The man looked at him. "I am, sir. I'd judge that you require the services of a doctor rather than those of a minister of the gospel."

Brandon remembered then how his reflection had looked in the horse trough and how the telegraph operator had reacted at sight of his battered face. He said, "Don't fret yourself over that. I want you to marry us."

Gail drew in a startled breath, and the preacher looked from Brandon to Gail. Whatever the man read in her face stiffened his own. "Is this your wish, too, miss?"

"No," Gail said firmly. "It isn't."

"I can have no part in this," the preacher said. He wedged himself deeper in his chair.

Several means of persuasion shuttled wearily through Brandon's mind, and he chose the one that called for least patience. He'd got beyond patience in the wagon yard. He lifted his gun from its holster and said, "The hell with arguments. Will you get your book and get to work with it?"

The preacher stood up, a man torn between conscience and the flesh. He swallowed hard and said, "Now, see here—" and let the words trail off. Brandon waggled the gun and felt a stir of amusement, his thought being that the situation was hindside to; when you had a gun at a wedding, it was usually trained on the bridegroom, not on the preacher. From the corner of his eye he saw Gail standing stiff and remote, understanding his intention now but not quite believing, if he were any judge. The preacher was both a terrified man and an angry one, but not angry enough to itch for martyrdom.

His wife stood by the door, her hands clasped before her and her broad face speculative. She said, "You go ahead and marry them, Abner."

Brandon looked at her, not expecting such an ally, and he decided it was not fear that had swayed this woman to intercede. The preacher stood up with a shrug and picked from a pigeonhole of the huge desk a small black book. He thumbed it with nervous hands but found the right page through long familiarity. He said in empty tones, "Stand together. Now take her right hand."

Brandon cased his gun and reached and got Gail's hand. He expected her to show fight, but her hand lay limp in his. He felt remote from what was happening, and he harked up a memory of the hotel room and Sam Whitcomb's emphatic order, but still he could not grasp the reality of here and now. He had a fleeting reluctance. He heard the preacher's voice drone away, but he did not look at Gail. He was conscious of faded carpeting and window curtains that had once been flour sacks and a homemade table holding the largest Bible he'd ever seen. The preacher was boniness and a voice; the preacher's wife's ample presence was dominant in the room; Gail stood stiff beside him. He answered the questions that were put to him. The preacher had forgot to ask their names beforehand and so stumbled at the questions. "Do you, er, miss, take this man to be your lawfully wedded husband?" Brandon heard Gail's small "Yes."

There was some awkwardness about there being no ring. "It isn't required," the preacher said hastily when Brandon stared at him. Finally the preacher closed his book. "I now pronounce you man and wife."

Brandon turned and drew Gail to him and kissed her. She did not respond to his lips, but she did not avoid them. The kiss hurt, for McCoy's knuckles had played havoc with his mouth. Brandon stepped back from her.

The preacher's wife had lifted a corner of her apron and was dabbing clumsily at her eyes. She said, "Don't mind me. I do this every time Abner ties a young couple together. I just can't help it. The marryings are even harder on me than the buryings." She came forward and put her big arms around Gail and held Gail close. She crooned at Gail's ear.

Brandon said to the preacher, "I want this in writing." The preacher slumped down at his desk and worked on a form with his pen. Brandon folded the paper and tucked it away and laid money on the desk. The preacher looked at him unhappily, his lips twitching with words unspoken. Then the preacher looked at his wife and held silent. The woman opened the door. Brandon got Gail by the elbow again, and they passed through the doorway and went along the walk toward the buggy.

Ten minutes since they'd come up this same walk, Brandon judged. Maybe fifteen.

He handed Gail up into the buggy and climbed to the

seat beside her and unwrapped the reins. Again he had
to stumble over Halliday's suitcase and was thus reminded of it. He said, "I suppose you've got all the
clothes you'll need. There's still this one suitcase to drop
off. And I want to get my horse."

She said in a small voice, "Do you think for one minute you can make this ridiculous business stick?"

He said grimly, "I can make it stick for a lot of minutes. Sure, you can get the marriage annulled. That's
what the woman whispered in your ear, isn't it? The
preacher will back your claim that it was a forced marriage. But you'll have to get away from camp first, and
you'll have to go all the way to the territorial capital at
Helena. Meantime, you can't marry anybody else."

She said, "If my father had asked you to throttle me,
you'd have done that, too, I think."

He shrugged. "I don't know. He didn't say anything
about that."

She said angrily, "You are absolutely the most insuf-
ferable man I've ever met!"

He grinned. "Now is that any way for a bride to be
talking?"

He brought the buggy around and went clattering up
the street. He drove between the facing rows of false
fronts to a stop before Mountain's headquarters, and
here he climbed down and reached in for Halliday's
suitcase. He had his back to the doorway as he did this.
Gail had sat stiff beside him on the short ride, her hands
clasped in her lap, her eyes straight ahead. A sudden
flash of expression on her face was his warning, this and
her quick *"Holt!"* and he flung about to see Halliday in
the doorway, a gun in his hand and his feet planted wide
apart.

"Brandon!" Halliday said.

Whether the man had seen the buggy stopped before
the preacher's house and thus guessed what had hap-

pened, Brandon couldn't know. But he saw Halliday as a man goaded by pride and jealousy to a fury beyond control; there was no sense in the man's face. He heard Halliday curse him; he saw the wildness in Halliday's eyes, and that gun was the biggest thing in the world. It spiked Brandon where he stood.

Gail cried, "No, Kirk! No!" but it was a feeble straw to stem the tide of the man's fury.

Halliday cursed again, with a more virile oath than Brandon had supposed the man commanded. Brandon moved then. He had one hand on the suitcase; he lifted the suitcase and shouted, "Here it is!" and flung it at Halliday. He saw it strike the man's huge chest and drive Halliday backward. He saw Halliday's arm swing up in an instinctive gesture to protect himself. Brandon had counted on this. The gun exploded, but the bullet went upward. Brandon made his leap. He got into the doorway and was upon Halliday; he drove the man back against the counter where the telegraph instruments stood. He grappled for Halliday's wrist and got hold of it and twisted hard. He heard the gun drop. He stepped back from Halliday and kicked at the gun and sent it spinning across the floor.

Brandon said, "That's all, Kirk."

Halliday stood with his face inflamed and his great chest heaving, but sanity had come back into his eyes. He lifted his hands and let them fall. He said, "This is an unfinished fight, Brandon."

"Some other day," Brandon said. He walked to the fallen gun and picked it up. He looked at the startled operator behind the counter and said, "Catch," and tossed the gun to him. He walked from the office, stepping over Halliday's suitcase.

He'd expected that from this interlude Gail might have seized a chance to flee, but she still sat in the buggy. He looked up the street toward the Hogshead and wondered where Champ McCoy had been toted and if he'd yet come awake. The fight with McCoy seemed like something that had happened last week. He got his piebald from the hitchrail and tied the mare behind the buggy and climbed back into the seat. Again he had to turn the buggy around, but soon he had it rolling back along the street. Beyond the town, he struck due north, following the telegraph line.

Gail said then, "I thought you might underestimate what he can do with a gun, since he's an Easterner. I've seen him at target practice."

He said, "Twice you tried to keep us apart—once in the wagon yard and once just now."

"The first time wouldn't have been a fair fight," she said. "You had just been through one battle, and it showed plainly on you. The second time was different. You had a gun, too, but that only meant that one of you was going to end up dead. Maybe both of you. I didn't want that."

He turned this over in his mind and found some strange satisfaction in what she'd said; she had showed herself fair-minded in her thinking and quick of judgment, and he liked that. He stole a glance at her and saw that she was again as stiff-faced as she'd been after the stop at the preacher's. Remembering what had happened there, he was not a proud man. He had used a strength against which she'd had no defense. He pushed this thought away.

Presently he laughed. "I was going to speak to Halliday about some insulators," he said. "Trouble is, he never gave me a chance."

She said unhappily, "Every thought you have is for Sam Whitcomb. I suppose if I were a natural daughter, I'd be proud that any man is so loyal to my father. But I wonder what makes you so."

He was silent for a time; he had carried a certain

knowledge for seventeen years, and sometimes he'd grown tired of carrying it about tight-locked. Jake Fargo had once guessed about it, coming close to the truth. He glanced now at Gail and said at last, "In Texas, after the war, I knew a boy named Buck Elliot. Yankee troops were stationed in our town, and they locked up Buck's father in the courthouse. Old Judge Elliot, he was. Buck was sixteen; I was fourteen. A pair of crazy kids. We figured to challenge the Yankee major to a gun fight on the street. We drew straws to see who'd do the job. I won."

Her interest was aroused. She turned her face toward him, her eyes grave. "And you did the shooting?"

He shook his head. "I was posted on the street, waiting for the major to show. I was holding the gun behind me. A stranger came along, and his eyes were sharp. He looked at me and smiled and said, 'Mighty big gun for a young lad, isn't it?' He had the cut of a Yankee, and I pegged him as some damn carpetbagger come in, but he had a way about him. After we'd jawed a bit, he got the whole story from me in spite of myself. Then he gave me a talk about how foolish it was to keep fighting a war that was over. He was in Texas to string a telegraph line, he said. He had a job for a boy just my size. He was leaving for his camp right away, and there was room in his wagon for me."

"Dad!" she said, understanding.

"Sam Whitcomb."

"So you never braced the Yankee major."

His mouth tightened. "Buck Elliot did that the very next day. Put a bullet in the fleshy part of the man's arm. I heard about the trial afterward. Buck talked up big, like a man. They gave him twenty years in a military prison, which is what I'd have got. I know about those military prisons; I talked to enough Johnny Rebs

who had a taste of them. All that was seventeen years
ago. So, you see, I've got three more years to serve."

She stared at him, her eyes wide and holding something akin to both sadness and anger. "You've believed,
then, that you owe my father twenty years of your life?
You've stood by him all this time for that reason?"

"Could there be a better one?"

She only shook her head. She held silent for a long
time in which the clatter of buggy wheels and the constant clop of the horses' hoofs became loud. He looked
out upon Montana's openness, remembering again that
raw and dusty Texas plain.

Finally she said, "Till now, I think I have half hated
you. Now I feel sorry for you instead. I would rather that
I hated you. Can you understand that?"

He looked down at his fists holding the reins; his
bruised knuckles hurt from the tightness of his grip.
"Yes," he said. "I guess I can."

14

CAME DOMINGO

In the broad sweep of the Valley of the Three Sisters,
Mountain's late campfire made a beacon that drew
Brandon across the last dark miles. Gail had fallen
asleep, sagging against his shoulder, and he was a
moody man, and alone, driving in the night. He had
told his tale to her and so unlocked himself, but he'd got
no balm from this. He had only harked up the old pain
of remembrance; and it lay heavily, greater than her
weight against him. Yet her presence was also constant,
and he was deep-stirred by it and thus reminded of the
strangest of all things, that she was now his wife. He
faced this reality and found it hollow.

She came awake when they were challenged by the outer guards, and he heard the quick intake of her breath as full knowledge came to her of her whereabouts. Probably she had expected to find Kirk Halliday with her, until she had remembered. Brandon felt her move away from him. He drove on until he was nearly into the rim of the firelight, and here he stiffly dismounted and gave his hand to her. He lurched like a drunken man. Piling a long buggy ride onto what Champ McCoy's fists had done to him made all his muscles alive with agony.

Jake Fargo moved up, a man plainly worried. He said, "You were gone a lot longer than I expected. Say, ain't that Miss Whitcomb with you?"

Brandon had already gauged how far the camp had moved northward since he'd left and so was pleased by the day's work. He nodded to Fargo's question. "Rig up one of the small tents for her, Jake."

Fargo asked, "How long will she be staying?" He was not happy about this.

Brandon remembered what Gail had said when he'd first taken her away from Halliday. "Till tomorrow. Maybe the day after. Maybe the day after that. How do I know?"

Fargo moved closer and squinted hard at Brandon. "What the hell happened to your face, Holt?"

"A round with Champ McCoy," Brandon said. "Will you get that tent ready, Jake?"

"Sure," Fargo said and made off.

Brandon turned toward Gail. She stood round-shouldered with weariness, and he said in a gentle voice, "Would you like something to eat while you're waiting?"

"Later, perhaps."

"I'll have Jake bring something to the tent."

Fargo came back shortly to announce that the tent

was ready. He indicated where it stood, and Gail moved away. Brandon realized that he had not eaten since breakfast, yet he had no real appetite now. Something had gone sour, spoiling his taste for all things. But tomorrow would be another day of work, so he moved to the cook's wagon and got a plate filled. He ate slowly and morosely. Some of the crew were still up, and he could feel their eyes on his battered face. Well, Jake had the answer and could pass it around. He finished with the food and built up a cigarette, but the smoke got into the cuts on his face and stung, and he soon ground paper and tobacco under his heel. He walked away from the firelight.

Someone had unharnessed the horse from the buggy and taken this animal and the piebald to the rope corral. Gail's suitcase was still in the buggy. Brandon took the suitcase and carried it to her tent. Light glowed dimly behind the canvas. He called her name softly.

"Yes," she said. She opened the flap and stood with her face tilted so that she might look up at him; she appeared less tired than when she'd climbed from the buggy. She was there before him, full-bodied and sultry as she'd been that first night in Whitcomb's private car. She looked at him expectantly, not voicing the question as to why he was here, and her soft fragrance seemed almost to reach out to him. He put his hand toward her and saw fear show quickly in her eyes. He remembered Sherm Lucas at Hashknife's cabin then and was ashamed, deeming himself no better than Lucas.

He said, "Here's your suitcase," and set it at her feet.

In his own tent, he thought of Sam Whitcomb. He opened the line to Salish and reported merely that Gail was at the camp. The Salish operator acknowledged the message and promised to deliver it to Sam at once. Brandon wondered whether Halliday was at headquarters. He thought of Halliday goaded past endurance and regretted giving the man such a rough day. He blew out his light a few minutes later and rolled into his blankets.

Sleep came slowly. He thought of Gail in that yonder tent and reflected that this was a hell of a way for a man to be spending his wedding night. He remembered those few minutes in the preacher's parlor like something from a dream, and the forced marriage now seemed to him a brutal and stupid thing to have done. He had carried out Whitcomb's order and brought her here where she'd be out of mischief. He had kept her from skallyhooting off with Halliday and arranged the marriage as a hurdle to slow her. But remembering the fear that had stood in her eyes a short while ago, he had a sense of defeat, a feeling of having lost far more than he'd gained.

So thinking, he at last fell asleep.

She was about when he came to the breakfast fire next morning. She wore the riding outfit she'd worn that night at Hashknife's line cabin. She gave him a cool nod, no more than that. He was soon busy at lining out his crew, and shortly he was up with the post-hole diggers, and she was lost to him somewhere in the welter of the camp behind. He wondered if he should hunt up Jake Fargo and tell him the full truth and put Jake to keeping an eye on her, but he decided against this. He could not hold her, really. A day, perhaps; a week— He had given advice to Sam Whitcomb about not trying to hobble her and forgotten to use that advice himself.

Damn it, but he felt like a board today; he had to keep moving to try to limber up! He wondered how Champ McCoy felt.

He saw Gail again in the afternoon, after the camp had been dismantled and the cooking outfit and tents moved up to the farthermost point the poles would reach that day. She had got one of the camp horses saddled, and she rode to where the post-hole diggers worked. Here she sat watching, her eyes alive with interest as each man finished his hole in turn and moved on up ahead.

Brandon came and stood by her stirrup. "A hot day for work," he said.

She shrugged. Her face held for him neither friendliness nor disdain; he might have been the cook or the teamster or any of the myriad men who worked on this project. She had reared a wall between herself and him that was invisible yet loomed higher than the hills. But she said, civilly enough, "The man I don't envy is the one who follows behind, trimming off tree branches that scrape the wire. The day is far too sultry for climbing."

His attention instantly quickened. "You've watched him work?"

She nodded.

The horse she rode looked to be long on both speed and bottom, and it was his immediate thought that if she'd fallen to the rear of the project, where the trimmer worked, there had been nothing to keep her from heading on south to Salish. This thought must have stood naked on his face, for she shook her head and said, "No, I wasn't tempted to bolt. You've probably got all of them keeping an eye on me. You'd have had your fun then, taking out after me and dragging me back. I shan't give you that pleasure. When I pick my time to go, the laugh will be on you."

He said stiffly, "This will surprise you. I'm the only man who knows why you're here."

He didn't look at her; he didn't want to see her triumph show, and he couldn't have told why he'd left himself so vulnerable. But he stood less ashamed for having told her, and he put his back to her and strode away about his business.

He was sure she'd be gone that night, but she was at

the supper fire. She was a merry one with the crew, bright as the flame; she laughed at their talk and had a cool reserve only for Brandon. He saw her go to her tent after she'd tossed her plate into the wrecking pan, and thereafter he sat cross-legged and hard-thinking by the fire, deaf to the talk of the men around him.

Later he arose and walked to Gail's tent. She had a lantern aglow inside, and her silhouette loomed big and lively on the canvas. She was brushing her hair. He called her name and heard her soft "Yes?"

He braced his legs apart. "If you want to leave tomorrow, I'll send a man with you to Salish."

Her shadow moved; he saw that she had flung back her head, but she didn't open the tent flap. "New orders from Dad?"

"My own notion," he said.

"Why?"

He lifted his hands and let them fall. He had no answer for her; he had only a feeling that to free her would be to free himself from the sense of wrongdoing he'd had since yesterday. In this notion, he supposed, lay some taint of disloyalty to Sam Whitcomb; he couldn't help that.

He asked, "Shall I tell one of the men to be ready to ride?"

"I'll let you know tomorrow," she said.

Again he went to his tent and lay sleepless, and his wonder was why she had not leaped at his offer. It came to him that he did not want her to leave; she had brightened the camp tonight as it had never been brightened before. He reminded himself that she was a willful one, born to trouble of her own making; but he also remembered her graver moods and the maturity she sometimes showed. Well, he would have her answer in the morning. He put her from his mind and burrowed deeper in his blankets.

But with the morning came Domingo—

That was after breakfast had been eaten and the crew had strung out. Gail had appeared at the breakfast fire, jaunty and gay and heedless of Brandon till he sought her out. Brandon put the question to her bluntly. "Are you heading for town?"

She shook her head. "I think," she said, "it will be more fun to slip away from you. To go as I please, rather than at your order."

He said, "But you can't go alone!"

"Yes, I can."

Anger rose in him, and he was astonished at its quick and heady rush. He wanted to reach out and take her by the shoulders and shake her hard. His thought was that Sherm Lucas prowled out yonder somewhere, and fear put a brassy taste in his mouth. But still the surprising thing was his anger. He said, "In the name of sense, Gail, think before you do anything foolish." He walked away from her and heard her laughter follow him.

Later, when he'd joined the wire stringers, Domingo came riding up.

The black was mounted on that big horse Brandon had delivered to Boxed T, and he showed a high excitement. The guards had raised a shout that brought Brandon running; and when he saw the wet flanks of the horse and the tired slump to Domingo's huge shoulders, he asked, "What is it, Captain?" But even then he knew, somehow, what the answer would be. Clear in his memory was his talk with Ellen Templeton in Boxed T's yard and the fear she'd voiced that day. Her fear had been with him ever since, submerged by other troubles; it rose now and engulfed him.

Domingo said, "Lucas attacking the place, suh."

Work had stopped. Men gathered around the two of them, pushing and jostling and voicing their questions. Gail was here, too. She looked at Domingo and lifted a hand as a sign of remembrance. Brandon asked, "Is the place under siege?"

Domingo nodded.

"How did you get through?"

"I was riding the high-lonesome last night. Early this morning, I see them from the rimrock, suh. Lucas's men all 'round the house. No use to fight through that line. I came here."

"How many men in Lucas's bunch?"

"Five, near as I could count."

Brandon stepped up to the saddle of his piebald. "I'll go back with you." He looked about until he spied Fargo's whiskery face in the crowd. "Take over here, Jake. Get these men back to their work."

Domingo turned stolid as an idol, but his eyes showed disappointment. "I'd hoped you'd fetch yo' men."

Gail had worked her way to Brandon's stirrup. She reached up and tugged at his sleeve. "You mean you're going alone?"

"I owe Boxed T something," he said. "We had it out the night I got beholden to them. It's a personal thing. The job of this crew is to put up telegraph poles."

She tilted her head toward Domingo. "I owe this man something myself. Holt, take the crew!"

"No," he said. "I know what I'm doing, believe me. I go alone." He looked at her; she still stood close by, yet he felt as though she'd moved miles away from him; she had moved far beyond his reach.

"Nothing will jar you from your notion?" she asked.

He shook his head. "Nothing."

"How long will you be gone?"

He looked out across the land. "Three hours, I suppose. An hour to get there, an hour to get back. That leaves time for whatever trouble there is." He looked at Domingo. "Let's get going. Do you want a fresh horse?"

Domingo's eyes moved across the gathered men, and

he lifted his big shoulders and let them fall. He said, "Miles left in this one, suh," and neck-reined the mount about.

Brandon picked his way through the gathered men and swung about in the saddle. "Get back to your work!" he shouted. "We're only a couple of weeks from deadline." He knew he was making the crew the object of an anger that he really felt toward himself. He faced forward and drew up beside Domingo, and they galloped stirrup to stirrup.

No time for talking on this ride. No chance, with the thunder of hoofs in a man's ears and the breeze of his own making to flatten the words back into his mouth. Four days now since he'd last ridden to Boxed T, but the distance was four days shorter, and that difference was measurable by poles set and wire strung. No sun today; the sky spread gray and sullen, and the clouds were piled high above the peaks. That rainstorm would make it yet.

At first flat country, flower-carpeted and endless. Then rough land of tortured trees. And ahead the rimrock. But always there was a shadowy saddlemate, an invisible one, a feeling that this time loyalty had been carried so far that it had turned into something else. It made a man's thinking darker than the sky; it gnawed at him like a wood tick.

A mile this side of where the land dropped away, they stopped to breathe their horses. Brandon got down to adjust the cinch. Domingo sat his saddle, a remote spirit and a sad one, not looking at Brandon, not delivering a judgment. At last Brandon said explosively, "Damn it, man, I'd have fetched them all if there'd been any real need!"

Domingo shrugged.

"But you said there were only five in Lucas's bunch," Brandon persisted. "That tallies with the count after we put two in jail and left one dead at the cabin. McCoy must be the fifth man. Ellen told me there were five in Boxed T's crew, not counting you. Templeton can handle a gun, can't he? When you and I ride down, there'll be eight against five." He climbed back into the saddle. "The two of us should tip the balance."

Domingo said, "Boxed T got no crew, suh."

This hit Brandon like a fist. *Got no crew!*"

"Miss Ellen laid them off a week ago, 'ceptin' me."

"Why, man? Why?"

Again Domingo lifted his shoulders and let them fall. "Happen after that night you met Miss Ellen up on the rim. You had some talk with her about how the crew gonna be outlawed if they fight the telegraph. She knew they fight if Colonel Templeton ask them. So she pay them off and send them away, suh."

Now Brandon remembered how deserted the ranch had been four days ago when he'd returned Domingo's horse, and suddenly sweat was cold on his skin. *God!*" he said. He looked back to the south, across the distance they'd covered. "Why in hell didn't you tell me at camp?"

"You the only one owe anything to Boxed T."

"Yes," Brandon said, and saw himself trapped by his own stubbornness. This made for him the bitterest moment he'd known. When you clung so hard to stubbornness, even though you called it loyalty, you had to be right always; you were allowed no wrong guesses. That was the price you paid, and it was too high; it had always been too high.

Again he looked to the south; he measured the distance to camp. "We'll have to go on," he said.

They touched spurs to their mounts and held to a gallop until they were nearly to the rim. Then they pulled down to a walk. Brandon listened hard for the sound of guns, but silence held. This worried him, and his nagging thought was: *Too late! Too late!* They eased up to the drop-off and looked down upon the sprawling buildings; and Brandon sagged in his saddle, sick and empty with the suddenness of relief.

Only peace dwelled below. The ranch yard drowsed beneath the sullen sky; a few horses stood idly in the corrals. But even at this distance Brandon could make out Colonel Templeton in the rocker on the porch, and when he peered harder, he saw Templeton's Winchester leaning against the porch railing. No other human showed but Templeton. The man was precisely as he'd been when Brandon had last seen him, four days ago; and something rose in Brandon that turned his voice hoarse. "They've beaten them off!" he said. "Damned if they haven't beaten them off!"

Domingo, too, was peering, hunched forward in his saddle as intent as any crouched panther. He said slowly, "I dunno. I just dunno," and Brandon wondered what jungle instinct put doubt in this big man.

He picked the same place to descend that he'd chosen the other day, and Domingo followed. Brandon heard rock roll beneath the hoofs of their horses. He could not see Domingo, but he could still feel the grave doubt of the black. Then it struck Brandon. A girl and an addled old man. How had these two turned back five such as Sherm Lucas and Champ McCoy and their men? But yonder sat Templeton with his rifle, making a picture that spoke of victory. And so Brandon rode on.

He had an odd thought then. He wished to hell the sun were out and shining. The day seemed now to press against him and hold its own dark foreboding, like the silent presence of Domingo.

15

DARK HOUR

Somewhere in that descent it came to Brandon how it might have been at Boxed T. The iron box was the key —the box of valuables which Templeton had once kept in the Salish bank. That box was what had brought Lucas here to lay siege; and Ellen, seeing the face of defeat, had given Lucas the box, and thereafter Lucas had shaken the dust of the ranch. Figure it that way, and you could understand why Boxed T now lay silent and deserted, with no danger showing in the yard. Yet Brandon was not completely satisfied with his conclusion and so found no real comfort in it. He rode on.

Smoke from the ranch-house chimney, a lazy lift of it, as though Ellen might be keeping a coffeepot warm. Horses switching their tails in the corrals. A hen scratching with no real enthusiasm at the hard-packed yard.

At the foot of the slope, Brandon could see that Templeton wore range garb. He'd had no time to dress in Confederate gray for the little war that had come to his doorstep. On level ground and walking the piebald steadily toward the house, Brandon now saw jagged stars in the window behind Templeton. Forty-fives had torn those holes in the glass. He remembered the night that Domingo's rifle had smashed at a window in Sam Whitcomb's private car, routing Lucas and McCoy.

He kept his eyes on Templeton's lean face. Templeton neither smiled nor frowned; the man made no sign of noticing them; and Brandon might have thought him dead, propped there in a chair, but the colonel's eyes were alive. Templeton watched them as intently as though he were memorizing them. As on that other visit here, Brandon kept his hands in sight, not knowing the temper of the man before him. The hen, almost under the piebald's hoofs, squawked and went fluttering around a corner of the porch.

Brandon advanced to the exact point he had reached when he'd returned Domingo's horse to this ranch. He pulled up and saw from a corner of his eye that Domingo was nearly beside him. What dark thoughts rode Domingo? Irritation touched Brandon; he wanted to be done with mystery. He asked, "What happened here, man?" putting the question to the colonel. Templeton rocked gently, not giving him an answer; and Brandon saw Ellen then.

She'd appeared in the open doorway to Templeton's right; she stood framed in that doorway, and the first thing Brandon noticed was how ghostly her face showed. The second thing was that she wore a holstered forty-five, just as she had the last two times he'd seen her. The gun reassured him. Her lips moved, but no words reached to him, and he had the feeling that he had suddenly gone deaf. But he felt a new surge of relief, for he knew now that his real fear had been that Lucas had come and gone, taking not only the iron box but Ellen as well. The fear had been one Brandon had not openly faced until it stood dispelled.

He swung down from his saddle, not waiting to be bidden. He let the reins drop, anchoring the piebald. Just then Domingo roared out a single wild word. *"No!"*

This brought Brandon half around. He saw Domingo jerk out his handgun and raise it; he saw Domingo's arm come up with the gun, but something moved across Domingo's broad black face, and Domingo tossed the gun to the ground. Brandon saw Sherm Lucas then. The man was a shadowy figure in the doorway, only the white flash of his teeth plainly showing. He stood directly behind Ellen, and that closeness was what had altered Domingo's judgment and taken the fight out of him. It also stayed Brandon's own hand.

Lucas had a gun on them. Lucas said, looking straight at Brandon, "You can shed yours, too, bucko," and Brandon gingerly lifted his gun from its holster and let it drop.

Lucas said, "Come in here. Both of you."

Something stirred in Brandon that was more rage than fear. He had smelled this trap but not quite sharply enough; he had walked into it like a blundering steer into a slaughterhouse. He could remember all the signs that had been there for the reading, the fixed gaze of Templeton, the soundless words of Ellen. He set his boot to the porch step and heard saddle leather creak and Domingo move to his side. He climbed the steps and felt Templeton's eyes. On Templeton's aristocratic face a great sorrow lay.

"You see," Templeton said, "I couldn't speak. Because of Ellen."

Brandon said, "It's okay."

Now he saw the dark stain of blood on Templeton's shirt, over the colonel's right ribs, and the slight bulge that showed that Templeton wore a bandage beneath his shirt. Casualty of war. Brandon faced the door. Lucas had his gun in his right hand; he put his left arm around Ellen's waist and pulled her back against him and backed with her deeper into the house. Brandon came in, Domingo behind him. In the big room in which Brandon found himself, a man stood on either side of the front window. Another was posted in a far corner. Champ McCoy sat sprawled in a chair.

Brandon recognized one of the men by the window. The fellow had been in Hashknife's line cabin. The other two Brandon had never seen close up. McCoy looked more battered than he had in the dust of Salish's street; his smile had lost its brightness; it was only a movement of the lips and a pull of wrinkles at the corners of his eyes. He said, "Ah, Brandon, it's good to see you. Pull up a chair and make yourself at home. Take the handiest one. Don't tire yourself."

But it was a long table toward which Brandon looked, for upon it sat that black security box fastened with a tiny padlock. This room was a mingling of Kentucky and Montana; it held plush furniture and rawhide-bottomed chairs, the elegance of the South and the makeshift contrivings of a raw frontier. A piano stood in one corner, and even in so taut a moment Brandon wondered how it had come, what river-boat deck had creaked under its weight, what freighter had cursed so bulky and frivolous a load on the stubborn passes. Upon the wall a banjo clock marked off the minutes, making a loud clamor.

Lucas said, "Bring the old fellow in here, too," and one of the men moved from the window. Lucas had released Ellen and stepped a pace away from her. He stood holding his gun idly, his dark face pleased. Templeton came in, herded ahead of the man who'd gone after him. Templeton looked weary and old, and Brandon judged that the man had lost much blood from his wound. The colonel carried his Winchester. He leaned it against a wall.

"Empty," he said.

"Mine, too," Ellen said in a dead voice, and Brandon saw now that her cartridge belt had been stripped of shells. He began to understand how the trap had been set.

Templeton turned to Lucas. "Would you mind if I went to my room and lay down?"

Lucas was instantly a suspicious man, saying sharply, "I want you where I can watch you!"

Brandon said, "Can't you see he's out on his feet? There's no fight left in him, and no scheming."

Lucas shrugged. "One of you boys keep an eye on his bedroom door."

Templeton moved to a door leading off from this room. Here he paused and looked about at the assembled men. He drew himself stiff and held his shoulders back, and fury stood strong in his eyes. Thus Brandon judged him to have a full grasp of the situation but no power left to pit against it. Templeton was a weary and wounded one, gone down to defeat; but he said clearly and firmly, "You're a bunch of mongrel dogs. You are not fit even to be guerrillas. Another day I will rout the pack of you." He moved on into his bedroom with McCoy's laughter loud.

Brandon said, "Take twenty years off him, and you'd not have found him so easy to handle, Champ."

Lucas stared at Domingo. "We saw you on the rimrock this morning, damn you. Get over in a corner now and put your back to the wall. Maybe you'll live, if you do. Jay, keep an eye on him. And lift that bowie out of his boot top. That's right."

McCoy stretched out his legs and found his own relish in this moment. "Sure, and we figgered the black was going for help, and where would he go but to Mountain's camp? That made a scared man out of Sherm. He expected your whole crew to be at your heels. But we've known each other from a long time back, eh, Brandon? You'd not drag your men from a job with a deadline so close and the miles so many. But you'd come yourself, for you were in cahoots with this big black before. That was my bet."

"Well," Brandon said, "you won it." He was thinking that here was the prime fallacy of the set and stubborn way; it made you entirely readable to your enemy; it made you a trapped man in the end. He was done now with a thing that had ruled him for a long time.

Ellen said in her empty voice, "Dad got wounded when they rushed the house. They bandaged him up because they'd got the notion of baiting a trap for you,

Holt. He was to be out there with the rifle. At the last I was to appear in the door, also with a gun. You were to believe that all was well here."

Brandon said, "I was a slow one," meaning to comfort her. Even in this dark hour she looked beautiful to him; and he wanted to reach her with his thoughts, to tell her that no blame was hers. He saw her again as one akin to himself, long blind in loyalty but learning at last that loyalty has many faces. She had let Boxed T's crew go.

Lucas said, "We've got to get moving. One of you boys get our horses out of the barn and bring them around front. Saddle a Boxed T horse for the girl. She's coming, too." He looked at Ellen, pure wickedness and a bold delight showing on him. "Maybe for a night, maybe for a week. You had your chance to call the dance a different way. But you shot at me when I showed a lantern on the rim. I hope there'll be that much fight in you when we make camp. I'll like that."

Brandon said in a flat and terrible voice, "You can find no trail so twisted I won't be able to follow it, Lucas. There'll be no mountain big enough for you to hide behind. Just remember that, before you drag her out of here."

Lucas laughed. "Hell," he said, "you'll be dead."

McCoy said, "My frolic first, Sherm," and came out of the chair, his battered face smiling. He drew his gun but put it in his left hand. He walked toward Brandon and dug at Brandon's ribs with the gun, then made a fist of his right hand and, still smiling, slammed that fist at Brandon's face. Brandon pulled his head aside, and McCoy's knuckles grazed against his cheek and caromed off his ear, filling his head with a great roar. Brandon's feet went out from under him, and he sat down heavily.

"Get up!" McCoy roared.

Brandon pulled himself slowly to a stand, holding tight to temper, knowing that temper could now be his death. He saw McCoy's fist lift again, but he heard Lucas say fiercely, "Quit it, Champ! Quit it, I say. I want him conscious for what I've got for him." McCoy's great chest heaved, and his eyes were savage, but he stepped back.

Lucas said, "Time to be getting out of here. Hasn't anybody started for those horses yet? Wrap up that iron box in a slicker, Champ; we'll pry it open later." He looked at Brandon and showed a feline pleasure. "And now," Lucas said, "I'm going to put a bullet in you."

McCoy said, "Low, Sherm. In the belly. So he'll go down to kick on the floor."

Brandon said, "You're a sweet one, Champ," and he was remembering that once he'd wondered if there was sincerity in that great hulk. He recalled McCoy's looking up at him from the Hogshead's porch after Sherm Lucas had been clouted; he recalled McCoy's saying, "I never want to be as hard a man as you, Brandon." He now saw McCoy fully and so saw a steady, surging brutality, a dark soul hidden behind a smile and an easy way of speech. Nothing counted with McCoy but his own brute needs, and no man meant more to him than the moment held. He was the jungle from which Domingo had lifted himself; he was more savage than Lucas, really, and more dangerous, for Lucas was a man pulled by small vanities and so was the more human.

Lucas lifted his gun and spread his legs apart and looked across half the room at Brandon. This, too, had been a day marked down on the calendar since that afternoon in the rocks and that night before the Hogshead. Lucas began cursing him, low at first, his voice rising and the vileness pouring out. He was a minute at this, and another; he was a man flailing himself to the pitch where anger would justify him. Brandon read the mounting fury in the man's eyes and turned desperate. In this hopeless moment, he remembered Gail's asking him how long he'd be gone and his telling her three hours. A futile hope, that one. Not enough time. Not enough time—

Brandon said, "Get it done with," and found his triumph in the saying, knowing himself to be a cooler one than Lucas. He was conscious of the great bulk of Domingo tense in a far corner; he whispered in his mind for Domingo to do no rash thing. He was aware that Ellen stood apart from Lucas, but he could get no real glimpse of her. He had to keep his eyes on Lucas. All the others were thus riveted, too; even McCoy stood spellbound. The gun leveled and steadied in Lucas's hand; Lucas turned silent, spent from his cursing; and in the silence the banjo clock beat steadily on the wall. And then a gun exploded.

It made fury in the room. Sound beat against the walls and filled the corners, and powder smoke laid an acrid taint everywhere. Only Lucas moved. He turned around in a fast spin, his eyes stricken and his face contorted and his hands clutching for a hold on the air. His gun dropped from his hand, and he went down heavily and was dead.

Ellen had a gun in her hand, the one she'd carried in her holster. She swung it in a wide arc and cried, "Easy! All of you!" her voice near to hysteria. "This gun is loaded! Do you understand? It's loaded!"

Brandon broke free of the trance first, and moved. He got across the room and snatched at the gun McCoy wore. He stepped back so that he had every man within his range of vision. He said, "Domingo, take the rest of them!" and found that he'd shouted it. He saw Domingo move from the corner and go to the other men, one by one, and lift their guns. Ellen stood unsteadily on her feet, still clutching her own gun. From the bedroom, Templeton's voice asked weakly, "What happened?"

Ellen said, "The trouble's over, Dad."

Brandon moved to her and got an arm around her and said, "All over, Ellen."

She let her gun fall to the floor. "There was only one shell," she said. "I bluffed."

Brandon stared. "They only thought they'd unloaded the gun? They missed one shell?"

"I had it in my pocket," she said. "They were satisfied to strip my gun belt; they never thought to search me. I got the shell into the gun while Sherm was cursing you. It was that shell you gave me the night Domingo and I hauled you out of the rocks. The one you said to send if I ever needed help."

He shook his head. He was thinking how the need had been the other way around. He looked at the form of Sherm Lucas on the floor, shapeless as a bit of melted *cunjer* wax by a distant campfire. He raised his eyes to Domingo, and the black man looked at Lucas, too, and nodded. Domingo had got the three men lined against a wall. McCoy had slumped into the chair, his battered face empty. "One shell and a bluff," he said and began cursing.

Brandon said, "Domingo, herd all of them out of the house and tie them up somewhere. In a harness shed, maybe. Can you handle them alone?"

Domingo nodded and wagged one of the guns he'd confiscated. The three men moved sullenly toward the door leading to the porch. Domingo looked at McCoy, who pulled himself to his feet and joined them. Afterward Brandon urged Ellen toward the door. He got her to the porch and let her drink in the heavy air of this sullen day. He was silent beside her; he felt featherbellied from having stood so near to death.

Ellen said feebly, "My father needs a doctor."

"We'll get one soon," he said. "I'll ride back to camp and use the wire. Salish can get hold of Doc King and have him on his way in another hour."

"That's good," she said. She leaned her weight against him. Presently she began to weep. He let her cry; she was quiet about it; he wondered how many of those tears came from shock and reaction and how many were for Sherm Lucas. She had dreamed her dream and been in at its death; all the bright-burning things left a shadow when they were gone.

After a while he said, "Look," and she lifted her gaze and let it follow his to the top of the rimrock, where riders came pouring. They made a great clatter on the slope, a massed flurry of movement, and at their head rode Gail and with her was Jake Fargo.

"My crew," he said.

Ellen asked in astonishment, "You told them to follow you?"

"No," he said, "but I'm not surprised they've come." He knew then the fullness of the change today had wrought. "And I'm not displeased."

16

BROKEN LIGHTNING

Mountain's crew came off the slope and rode into the yard and swirled there, the horses milling. Hard-packed ground yielded to these many hoofs, and dust rose. In the chaos, Gail was the first to dismount; she slipped down and led her horse to the foot of the steps and looked up at Brandon and Ellen, and was voiceless. Brandon studied Gail's face, trying to read there some elation because she had found him safe. Excitement had given Gail a high color. She was plainly trying to absorb a dozen impressions at once, to read Boxed T's safety in what there was to see. She had no single reaction in this first moment—elation showed on her, yes, but also curiosity and the last tag end of fear—and thus there was nothing for Brandon alone. This disappointed him keenly.

He said, "All's well here now. But I'm glad you came." He saw Jake Fargo emerge from the group and come to a stand beside Gail. "Lucas is dead in the parlor. The rest of them are disarmed. Colonel Templeton was wounded and is in bed. He needs a doctor. We'll wire for King."

Fargo said, "The line's cut, Holt."

Brandon shook his head. "But I opened to Salish early this morning, just as a matter of routine."

Fargo's whiskery face puckered. "Then it was cut since. I tried checking on some supplies shortly after you left. That wire was dead as could be. The supplies came rolling in a little later, and the freighter said there'd been no dangling wire while there was daylight to see. Made me wonder if the old trick of cutting and splicing hadn't been worked. When I told Miss Whitcomb, she began to get really worried. She figured there might be a tie-up between the cut line and the attack on this ranch. She ordered us all to saddles, and we hit out for here."

Brandon made a fist. You thought that with Sherm Lucas dead and Champ McCoy prisoner you had the situation by the tail on a downhill drag, but there'd been one last fling in the enemy that you hadn't known about. Brandon became an angry man, and an impatient one.

"I sent Bruce to look for the break and make repairs," Fargo went on. "But there's an awful lot of miles of line to check, Holt. You know how hard it will be to find a splice."

"I know," Brandon said, lost in his own dark thinking. "Jake, tell a couple of the boys to move Sherm Lucas out of the parlor. Then you come with me."

Ellen said to Gail, "Won't you come inside where you can rest?"

Gail looked down at her skirts and began to beat the dust from them. Then she raised her eyes to Ellen. This was the first meeting of these two, and they gave each other a frank appraisal, and from it Brandon judged that they would be friends. They were strong, both of them, and warm, and each had been put to one test and another on this range. They had their differences of background, and one was dark and one golden, but they were drawn now toward each other. As Gail climbed the steps, Brandon brushed past her going down. He had this small moment of contact, and then he was on his way around the porch toward the barn.

In the ranch yard, he encountered Domingo. Domingo gave him a wide and toothy smile. Brandon remembered the night he'd asked Domingo how an obligation would stand between them. He had his answer in Domingo's smile.

Brandon said, "Got those four locked up, Captain?" When Domingo nodded, Brandon said, "Bring McCoy out." Domingo headed for the barn. Jake Fargo came running across the yard. Brandon shouted, "Find me a saddle rope, Jake." Fargo turned back toward Mountain's crew and returned bringing Brandon a lariat.

Jake asked, "Shouldn't we be heading back to camp?"

"A first thing first," Brandon said. He hefted the rope in his hand.

Domingo came out of the barn, pushing McCoy ahead of him. McCoy's hands were bound behind his back. He lurched along, a huge, shambling hulk with nothing left in him but truculence. His square face tightened up at sight of Brandon; his eyes gave Brandon the fullness of his hate.

Brandon asked, "Where did you cut our line, Champ?"

McCoy said, "What the hell you talking about?"

Anger rose in Brandon and swept all patience away. He said grimly, "Fetch him over to yonder corral gate," and strode across the yard to stand beneath the crossbar over the gate. McCoy looked at the rope Brandon carried, and some intimation turned McCoy's eyes wary. He stood stubbornly until Fargo gave him a hard shove. When the three came up, Brandon was holding the rope in listless fingers, but his jaw ached from tightness.

Brandon stared at McCoy's battered face. "You bragged about how well you knew me, Champ. You made a right guess that when Domingo came to my camp for help I'd ride with him and leave my crew at work. But it might have crossed your mind that I'd wire Salish and tell them of the attack. Every rancher within reach would have been willing to ride in a posse against Lucas. So you took care of that." He shook out the noose and sent it spinning up and over the crossbar. The rope fell and struck McCoy's shoulder. Brandon lifted the noose and settled it around McCoy's neck. "Who's guessing right this time, Champ?"

McCoy began cursing.

Brandon said in a flat voice, "We need that wire open, and fast. You'll tell us where that cut was made." He jerked at the rope and took the slack out of it. He leaned back, putting his weight on the rope until he had hauled McCoy up to his tiptoes.

Fargo said, "My God, Holt! We're not the law!"

Brandon said furiously, "Do you send for a sheriff if you meet a rattlesnake on a day's riding, Jake?" There was now nothing in the world for him but the need to break through McCoy's stubbornness. But he eased up on the rope, and McCoy's feet flattened against the ground.

"Talk, Champ!" Brandon said.

McCoy strangled and coughed until he had recovered his voice. But craftiness showed in his eyes. "How did we know this big darky would be free of the ranch and able to ride to a telegraph line?"

"You didn't, Champ. You were just guarding against any such slip."

"You damn fool!" McCoy roared. "The Negro will tell you we were here at dawn. How the hell could we have cut your wire this morning?"

Brandon pounced on this. "So you *did* know it was cut this morning! I hadn't told you *when*, Champ. But I'd figured out how you operated. You didn't cut the wire last night on your way here. We might have discovered the break too soon and repaired it. So you fixed it with someone to have the wire cut this morning. Not one of Lucas's regular bunch; they were all here. And not a saloon hanger-on you might have hired for ten bucks; that kind you couldn't have been sure of. Who did it, Champ? And where did you have him make the cut?"

"The hell with you!" McCoy said, but the defiance was only in his voice. He was a man backed into a tight corner, and his eyes showed fear.

Brandon got both hands on the rope again and tugged.

"Halliday!" McCoy shouted.

"Yes," Brandon said, and was somehow not surprised. He'd have put his heart into such a job. "Where, Champ?"

"About fifteen miles out of Salish the line passes through that first big clump of trees. A man could work there in broad daylight and never be seen. And you'd never have found the break."

"Because you had Halliday put in a splice," Brandon said. He let the rope drop. "Lock him up again, Captain."

McCoy's face knotted to complete hardness, and he began his cursing. At the end of this, he said, "I'm going to get you, Brandon, and I'm going to get Sam Whitcomb. It's a promise I'm making. Fixing Whitcomb will be for Consolidated, but getting you will be for my own pleasure. No man puts a rope around my neck. On some dark night, I'll be after you."

Brandon said wearily, "This time you'll not be able to swear you were back East in Consolidated's office while the frolic was going on. I'm glad to be done with you, Champ."

Jake Fargo expelled a long, harsh breath and looked like a man about to be sick. "I think you'd have bluffed him till his face turned black, Holt."

"Was I bluffing?" Brandon asked.

He turned and walked away. He came around the corner of the porch and climbed the steps and walked through the open doorway into the parlor. He at once saw that Sherm Lucas's body had been removed; a dark stain marred the carpeting. Gail sat alone in the room, her hands idle in her lap. She looked up at him, not speaking. He thought of the knowledge now his and remembered that Gail had not long ago been on her way to marry Halliday. The full truth must soon be hers, and he was sorry for that, but he could spare her now. So all he said was, "Where's Ellen?"

Gail nodded toward Templeton's bedroom.

Brandon walked inside. The colonel had been got out of most of his clothes and now lay beneath blankets; his face was white against the pillow, but his eyes opened. He was a warrior hauled down in battle.

Ellen sat beside the bed. Of her Brandon asked, "How is he?"

"Resting," she said. "He seems in no real pain, but I wish Jonathan were here."

Brandon said, "I've found out where the line was cut. I just stepped in to say I'm leaving now to have it repaired. Then we'll get word to King." He saw how much this day had taken out of her; she looked almost fragile, as though she would shatter if touched. He smiled. "Don't worry," he said.

He turned back toward the door, but Templeton called weakly, "One minute, sir."

"Yes?" Brandon said.

"I seem to owe you an apology, but I must ask your indulgence until my strength is greater." He passed his slim fingers over his face. "I know now that you have meant us no harm. On the contrary, you have been our ally. My daughter tells me that your force is at my door, come here to help rout those guerrillas. I have never held with their kind of warfare, no matter what flag they raised; they did our cause no real good in Missouri and Kansas. I'm also told that your telegraph line will now serve me by fetching Doctor King. I am convinced that you are no enemy of the Confederacy, sir. I shall instruct Captain Domingo that you are to have our fullest cooperation."

"Thank you," Brandon said, and it struck him hard that he need never again be sorry for Templeton. Queer how you stuck with the notion that such a man was to be pitied. Now he saw Alan Templeton in a new way; here was one who lived always in the past, and thus the past was not a thing done with and beyond reclaiming. For such a one there was no Appomattox, no sorry peace, no empty homecoming, no bitter finalities. Always the bright banner went forward, and the cause was not lost. Always the faith in victory held strong. Many men had less. Clearly seeing all this, Brandon said, "I've got to be riding now." He drew himself erect and raised his hand in a stiff military salute, and there was nothing ludicrous in the gesture.

"Ride well," Templeton said, and lifted his hand and let it fall.

Brandon stepped back into the parlor and would

have strode past Gail, but instead he paused. She had come here because of a worry that had included him; that much he'd gleaned from what Jake Fargo had said. He wanted to tell her that he was grateful, but something closed him out, something made of his new knowledge of Halliday. But this also held the one gift he could bestow upon her. He said, "I'm going all the way to Salish. I'll appreciate it if you'll stay at the camp until I get back. I'll make it by tomorrow at the latest."

Her face livened so suddenly that he wondered at her intuition. "Holt," she asked, "what are you hiding from me?"

He could make no answer, so left the room and the house. The crew stood waiting by their horses in the yard. He picked up the piebald's reins; and because the old habit still clung to him, he said, "Try to get a few poles set before sundown."

He skirted the crew and led his mount toward the slope. He knew now, having had that interlude with Templeton, that there was no life-and-death rush to get King; it was another matter, really, that would take him southward; and reluctance rose in him, pulling against a clear duty. He was just climbing to saddle when he heard his name called and Ellen came running after him. This was so much like the last time he'd left Boxed T that he was startled and for a moment had a sense of time turned back.

She reached him and stood by his stirrup and looked up at him. "I just had to thank you," she said.

"It's the other way around," he said, and remembered a gun's roar beating back from the parlor walls. "That was a close thing."

She shook her head. "It goes beyond what happened when Sherm had us trapped. I watched your face while you talked to my father just now. I saw you salute him. That was something more than humoring a crazy one."

Brandon said, "Yes. He doesn't need our pity."

Ellen's face softened. "I understand. When Sherm attacked this morning, I had a foolish hope that the shock of such a battle might jar my father from that old shock of long ago. Jonathan used to wonder if such a thing might work a cure. Now I know he will always be as he is. I have lived with his sickness for a long time. Now it will be easier to live with. That's what I'm thanking you for."

This left him awkwardly silent. Finally he asked, "Your crew? Have they quit the country?"

"They were hanging around Salish the last I heard."

"Round them up and bring them back," he said. "The trouble's done with. And another thing. If you want that box of valuables safe in the Salish bank again, I can take it with me."

She said, "That box contains Confederate bonds. Worthless paper."

Confederate bonds! He had to laugh, and he let the laughter come.

She looked down. "I could have told Sherm that long ago, but perhaps he wouldn't have come back to the rimrock. I kept hoping that soon it would be more than the black box that brought him. This morning it was too late to tell him the truth." She raised her eyes to him. "Now do you hate me?"

He looked at her; he saw in the slight quiver of her lips and the agony in her eyes how anxiously she awaited his answer. He could destroy her now with a word or the withholding of one. He touched his thumb to a button of his shirt and said, "Here's another who got his sense of values twisted. All of us deal in Confederate bonds sometime." He smiled. "I must ride now."

She was near to crying. "Ride carefully, Holt."

He knew now what she had wanted of him, and he would want, always, as much from her—a solid understanding between them, an unblemished respect. He bent from the saddle and got his arm around her and drew her close and kissed her. He was unmindful of Mountain's crew, who stood in the yard watching. Her lips clung hard to his for that brief moment; and this was their pact, their understanding. It held something gained and something lost.

He released her and separated the reins and evened them. He put the piebald toward the slant and rode upward, and at the crest he faced south and lifted the mare to a high gallop.

17

GUN SONG AT SALISH

Rain came while he rode the valley's openness, a soft and slanting rain that laid its peace upon the land. Brandon had then covered half the distance to camp. Soon the rain came hard enough to make him unlash his slicker from behind the saddle. All the yonder peaks were lost in woolly mist, and he rode in a shut-in world. He hunched his shoulders inside the slicker and tugged his sombrero brim low and let the piebald pick her unerring way. He rode like this across the last miles and presently saw the tents emerge out of the grayness. Vague movement there of those who'd been left behind. One of these challenged Brandon; Jake Fargo had thought to leave a guard posted. Brandon spoke up and moved on in and found the cook.

Dismounting, Brandon said, "I could use something to eat. I've got to get on to town."

The cook swept his arm to the north and asked, "What's been happening up there?" His voice held a frank disgust. "All my life I've been chained to pots and pans whenever there's any excitement stirring."

Brandon gave a brief report while the cook rustled grub for him, finding no pleasure in talking about the morning. After he'd eaten and had a cigarette, he went to his tent and tried to raise Salish by telegraph. Always a chance that the repairman had found the break and fixed it; but the line had no life. Brandon came out of the tent. He thought of changing to a fresh horse but decided against this. The crew had taken the best mounts; and the piebald looked frisky enough, and he was used to the mare's ways. He realized he was wasting time on these small efforts and small decisions, and faced again his own reluctance. He made an angry shrug. Then he rose to saddle and headed into the rain.

Not coming down so hard farther to the south. After the first miles he didn't really need the slicker; and when he rode out of the Three Sisters, the rain had slackened so that he could see a stretch of country. Shortly he made out a horseman ahead of him, slowly pacing the line. Drawing closer, Brandon recognized him as one of the crew. This was the fellow Fargo had sent in search of the break; he was one who'd been wounded the night McCoy and Lucas had attacked the camp. Doc King had ordered this fellow to Salish, but lately he'd rejoined the crew. Brandon, overtaking him, said, "A man should be a fish on a day like this, Bruce."

Bruce shook his head. "Better an eagle so he could fly along the wire." He was a weary one, dispirited by rain and futility. "Jake figured it might be a splice job. I've climbed twenty poles on the notion that the cut might have been made from one of them."

Brandon said, "You'd have kept climbing till you got tangled in your own whiskers. The cut was made between poles; the wire was reached from a tree. Champ

McCoy told me where to find it. Come along and I'll show you."

Bruce's interest quickened. "Then McCoy was at Boxed T. You got him cooled down?"

Brandon said, "We're finished with him."

They rode on together, and by late afternoon Brandon judged they must be near the place McCoy had mentioned. Remembering that this quest was based on so flimsy a thing as McCoy's word, he wondered if there might have been a last bit of craftiness left in McCoy. Then a clear picture came to him of the man's fear-stricken eyes, and he recalled how the rope had felt to his hands when he'd put his weight on it, and his surety returned. Peering through the rain, he saw a clump of poplars and mountain ash into which the line ran, so large a growth that they hadn't detoured around it when they'd put the wire through here. Riding into these trees, both men dismounted.

Bruce carried a pair of lineman's climbers and also a portable instrument and a length of ground wire. The climbers looked old enough to have been the original ones that obscure genius Smith had invented back in the 'forties. Bruce donned the climbers and went up a tree; he threshed about, showering raindrops on Brandon, who stood waiting. Presently Bruce called down, "I think I see the break from here." He came down and moved to another tree. He was a cheerful man now. He let the ground wire play out as he began climbing. Soon he shouted, "I can reach it."

Brandon said, "When you get the line open, tell divisional to find Doc King and send him to Boxed T. Colonel Templeton needs him. Got that?"

"Sure," Bruce said.

Brandon mounted and rode out of the trees and continued on southward. He rode at a steady gait, not punishing the piebald; he rode empty-minded. He'd had the need to find the break and fix it, and that had given him something to hold to. Now there was only the other chore, and he pushed the thought of it away.

No reading the time, not with the sun hidden. He measured time by the miles he put behind him. Now and then he sighted remembered landmarks from the days when he'd pushed the line northward. He found the wagon road and followed it. This again brought him near that nest of rocks where once he'd crouched under siege from Sherm Lucas and his men. Nearly a month ago that had been.

Rain put a different face on a world that had been familiar; and when he looked behind, he could see that it still pelted down hard in the valley. Mist held all the land from which he had emerged, the fog lying in gray streamers and the mountains gone. He faced ahead and supposed he should soon be sighting town; and when he peered, he made out a buckboard careening toward him. Doc King? Time enough for the break to have been fixed and the word to have started King north. He followed the road toward the buckboard; and when he got close enough to the wagon, he lifted his hand. King, sure enough.

"No use wearing out your whip, Doc," Brandon called. "The colonel will keep till you get there." He urged the mare alongside the buckboard.

Jonathan King sighed and relaxed on the seat. "The day operator was just going off shift when the message came through," he said. "I started as soon as he fetched it to me. What's happened?"

"Lucas hit at the ranch, and Templeton got a bullet along his ribs," Brandon said. He saw the instant concern that leaped into King's eyes, and he added, "Ellen's all right."

King said, "I'll get on."

But Brandon didn't nudge the piebald. He put his

speculation on King, remembering the talk they'd once had about Boxed T and its needs, and he asked bluntly, "Doc, did you ever declare yourself to her?" This startled King and so gave Brandon his answer. "Both of them up there need you," Brandon said. "Sherm Lucas died today. From a gun in her hand. I'd walk into that house and go straight to her and take her in my arms."

King stared in astonishment, then shook his head. Brandon saw a man who'd lived with his own special despair so long that it always lay just beneath his gaiety and showed on him in the unguarded moments.

"First there was Lucas," King said. "I told you about his coming to the rimrock with a lantern. Then you came here. She's talked about you a great deal. I got the notion that if you'd showed up first, she'd have given Lucas no time. It follows that you might be interested, too."

Brandon grinned wryly. "Maybe you haven't heard, Doc. Hell, I'm a married man."

He skirted the buckboard and rode on. With him he carried the remembrance of King's face, startled and perplexed but at last hopeful. This remembrance brightened the last of a gloomy day, but again there was something gained and something lost. He recalled how he'd judged Ellen's need at their parting at Boxed T; he wondered if he had been blind to something King had seen. He didn't know, and now he had sent King to her. He pondered this until he saw the lights of Salish in early evening and rode into the street.

An ugly town in the rain, Salish. A bedraggled town, gray and abandoned-looking, with mud everywhere and the boardwalks nearly deserted, and the log and clapboard as forlorn as a funeral. A few horses stood at hitchrails, their tails drooping, their heads down. A few wayfarers shouldered against the rain. One of these, cutting across the street toward a restaurant, Brandon recognized. This was the Mountain Telegraph man who'd been posted as guard in the hotel hallway outside Sam Whitcomb's door. Brandon shouted, "Sam all right?"

The man peered through the rain. "Sleeping, when I left him."

"He's alone?"

"I've only stepped out for a bite of supper. I'll be going right back."

Brandon moved on to Mountain's headquarters. Light shone through the glass, and rain lay in silver streaks along the glass. Dismounting, Brandon tied the piebald before the building and crossed the walk to shoulder into the single room. Halliday was the only man here. Brandon felt a tightness in his belly then, a last reluctance.

Halliday hoisted his big body out of the swivel chair before the pigeonhole desk and crossed to the counter. He had no smile for Brandon. He said petulantly, "What's going on up in the valley, man? The line's been dead most of the day. Now that it's open, the only message we've got is a garbled one for King. I've nearly gone crazy waiting."

Brandon said flatly, "Quit it, Kirk."

This held its warning for Halliday, and the impact of that warning showed on his face. For a moment Halliday's stare was startled, and then the surprise left him and he was wary, trying hard to read Brandon.

Brandon asked, "How long have you been working for Consolidated, Kirk? All day that's been gnawing at me. You fetched Jake Fargo whisky, when every man in the organization knows Jake is a bottle fighter. Still, you were new and might not have heard. But you were only roughed up a little, not really hurt, that day Lucas and McCoy snatched the payroll and Gail from your buggy.

Just what the hell did you expect to gain by working against Mountain?"

He watched Halliday closely; he expected him to show anger or make a try at bluffing. But Halliday merely shrugged.

"I'm a minority stockholder in Mountain," Halliday said. "A while back I had a chance to buy a considerable block of Consolidated stock. The stuff dropped, because Consolidated didn't look likely to get Montana business away from Whitcomb. With the price low, opportunity readily suggested itself to me. The defeat of Mountain will mean a small loss on my stock with that outfit, but nothing compared to what I'll recoup when Consolidated stock goes up again. It's simply business, you see."

"You admit all this?" Brandon asked, and was now the startled one.

"A confession?" Halliday shook his head. "Sooner or later it will be obvious that I own Consolidated stock. There's no law against buying it. Nor in being acquainted with Champ McCoy, who has been in the same town with me nearly a month. Where's your proof that I took any orders from him?"

Brandon felt sick. "And still you'd have married Gail if I hadn't stopped you!"

Again Halliday shrugged. "A man has to look to his future. Sam Whitcomb has had his back to the wall before and managed to fight through. But with my holdings in Consolidated and a wife who will someday own most of Mountain, I'll be fixed no matter which way the wind blows."

Here it was again, Brandon thought, the difference between himself and this man to whom telegraph building meant only a hope for profit. Now Brandon's anger came in a great rush. He said, "You had a gun here the last time. I'm of a mind to make you try for it.

Instead, I'm telling you to pack up and get out of Salish. I'll give you just one hour to be gone."

He turned away. He had his hand to the door when the Wheatstone began to clack out a message. S-A-L-I-S-H W-H-Y D-O-N-T Y-O-U R-E-S-P-O-N-D. The urgency of this brought him around, and he saw the dismay on Halliday's face, and knew this was a message that had come again and again, one that Halliday hadn't wanted him to hear. H-A-S B-R-A-N-D-O-N A-R-R-I-V-E-D T-E-L-L H-I-M M-C-C-O-Y E-S-C-A-P-E-D T-E-M-P-L-E-T-O-N R-A-N-C-H S-T-O-L-E H-O-R-S-E A-N-D H-E-A-D-E-D S-O-U-T-H A-C-K-N-O-W-L-E-D-G-E.

That was Jake Fargo at the key. That was Fargo desperately hurling the long lightning across the miles. And hearing the message, Brandon's streaking thought was of the time he'd spent at camp and in the clump of trees and on the roadside talking to King. Time enough for another to have reached Salish first and got himself a gun. Instinctively he dropped to the floor behind the counter. He heard Halliday's voice rise wildly. *"Mc-Coy!"* He heard the back door open and a gun blast, and knew now why Halliday had spoken so freely and where McCoy had waited, knowing that he, Brandon, would come.

He got on his hands and knees and worked his gun out of its holster. He came up like a jack-in-the-box; he came up firing. Wherever Halliday had kept his gun, it was now in his hand. Halliday had fallen back a few paces until he stood against the desk. Just inside the rear door McCoy stood, his smile showing. Halliday, lifting his gun, brought the barrel down to eye level; here was one trained to targets and thus careful about his shooting. Brandon saw in him the immediate menace and snapped a shot toward him. Halliday jarred to the impact. His face showed a vast surprise, and then his legs gave way. He sat on the floor with his mouth slack and no life in his eyes; he toppled over.

McCoy fired. Brandon felt the bullet tug at his sleeve. He shot at McCoy hastily—too hastily; he saw the door frame splinter beside McCoy. Brandon put the heel of his gun hand to the counter and vaulted over. He came at McCoy in a rush, remembering instinctively how McCoy had broken under stress that night in Whitcomb's private car. He counted on the core of cowardice in the man and saw fear cross McCoy's face now. McCoy turned and bolted through the back door. Brandon ran after him into the shadowy wagon yard with its piled supplies. No sign of McCoy.

Brandon paused in the sibilant rain, at once fearing ambush. He stood with his gun held ready, harking hard for some sound of McCoy. He stood for a full minute and another. He wondered if McCoy had fled the yard in panic and was now losing himself in the town; then full realization struck him.

Whitcomb! Sam alone—Sam, who'd been listed by McCoy this very morning as second when McCoy's chance came!

Running back into the office, Brandon vaulted the counter again. He lunged out through the front door, leaving it open. Few people on the boardwalk this rainy night; the gunshots had raised no furor. Brandon ran along the street to the Ballard House and came bursting into its lobby. He took the stairs two at a time and caught his boot toe in an edge of loose carpet and went sprawling. He got up and gained the hall and saw a lurching figure ahead of him. That figure swerved against Whitcomb's door and into the room. Brandon heard a gun speak.

He came into the room on McCoy's heels. Murk here, and the dim white shape of a bed, and the heavy smell of burned powder. Gun flame suddenly lighted the murk. Close, that one! Brandon made out the burly figure of McCoy in the flash and fired at McCoy and saw the big man dwindle before him. McCoy fell heavily. Brandon, still tasting fear, cried out frantically, "Sam?"

Whitcomb said, "Here." Brandon moved around to the far side of the bed, stepping over McCoy, and saw Whitcomb sprawled on the floor in his nightgown. "I rolled out of bed when he hit the door," Whitcomb said. "That's how he missed me. He was so excited he blazed at the pillow. I think this damn shoulder has torn open again."

Brandon said, "Let me help you." He cased his gun and got hold of Whitcomb and lifted him back onto the bed. Not much more weight to him than a sack of feathers. "Doc King's gone up into the valley, Sam. Let's have a look at that bandage." He fussed with the bandage; it showed a bright-red stain. He got it firmly into place again. "Hope that will do till King gets back. I'll send word to him." He looked at the shapelessness of McCoy and felt sick; there'd been too many dead men today. "Your guard should be back from supper soon. He'll move McCoy out of here. There's another dead one at headquarters. Halliday."

Whitcomb's face sharpened with interest. "He was in with Consolidated?"

"He did some of their chores. It was himself he really worked for, and he let the chips fall where they might. Tonight he framed up McCoy's chance at me. Halliday might have walked clear of that, but he made the mistake of backing McCoy's gun with his own."

Whitcomb shook his head. "Now I know why I never cottoned to him, Holt. There was a rotten spot there, always. Sooner or later it was bound to show." He reflected for a moment. "Poor Gail!"

"I've got to get word to camp," Brandon said. "Will you be all right, Sam?"

"Fine," Whitcomb said. His face softened. "Is Gail still up there?"

"Yes, Sam."

Whitcomb said, "I'd like her here, Holt. Especially if I've got to wait for this wound to heal again. Will you send for her in your message?"

"Sure," Brandon said. He looked at Whitcomb and smiled. He had wondered sometimes about his feeling toward this man, not knowing clearly how much of it was made from long servitude. But he had known how deep his affection lay when he had plunged along the boardwalk and climbed the stairs to this room with Mc-Coy just ahead of him. He said now, "I'll take care of everything, Sam."

He walked out in the hall and came down the stairs. He saw the startled clerk at his desk. He said to the clerk, "There was some trouble upstairs; you heard the shots. It's all over now."

When he came out to the boardwalk, the rain felt good against his face, and he stood for a moment with his face lifted. Tiredness rode his every muscle, what with the accumulated burden of all the hours and all the miles. But there was work to be done—a camp to be reassured, a doctor to be summoned, a daughter to be called to her father's bedside. And there'd have to be an inquest. He'd ask Salish law to hold the inquest tonight so he could get back to camp.

He walked along slowly, and it came to him that Mountain Telegraph had nearly made a clean sweep today, destroying all its obstacles but one. There was still terrain to be covered and time to be conquered; there was still the last of a race to be run.

18

DEADLINE

String wire, and you bed each night in a new place, and the distance from your last camp marks the miles you have covered that day. Not enough. Not ever enough. Drive deep into the valley, and on an evening you see the lights of Boxed T to the east, and the next night Boxed T's cattle graze beyond the rim of your firelight. Soon the land starts standing on its head; your crew works up an endless slope, and you grow frenzied because this is slow country, and you are now counting the time to deadline not in days but in hours. No sentries needed, for Sherm Lucas and Champ McCoy no longer ride by night and there is no threat from a last Confederate; it is only the face of the mountain that threatens to defeat you. Poles are easily come by, for timber is all around, but the other supplies have to roll the long miles from Salish. The brush fires burn, and you work with your men by flaring light, forgetting what it is to sleep, not caring about anything but the need to reach Warlock. You are nearing that boom camp, for you meet men on the mountain trails, bearded men, packs on back, who hurry forward with the prospector's eternal hopefulness. "We'll have a drink with you tomorrow," they shout, when they learn your destination; but the pack you carry is much heavier, and Warlock is many tomorrows away. Time is something beyond price, something clutched at and cherished. Not enough. Not nearly enough.

Thus Brandon fought the last miles. A week had gone by since he'd been in Salish; a second week sped after it. He'd kept the telegraph working between camp and town and so knew that Sam Whitcomb was held to his bed by orders from Doc King; Sam had done himself in, with that frantic effort to escape McCoy's bullet. Gail was with her father. She'd got Brandon's message from town and caught a ride to Salish with a freighter that very night. Somewhere in the darkness she and Brandon had passed each other; he'd started for camp late, after the inquest, and so had not seen Gail since the day he'd left her at Boxed T. Remembering Kirk Halliday dying against that pigeonhole desk, he guessed how it was with Gail these days and dreaded the hour when he must face her again. Nor had he seen Ellen. She, too, stood by a sickbed, he supposed; and now the wire was far past Boxed T.

July blazed down upon the mountainside, and the crew fought heat as well as terrain. Belated rains came to lash the camp; the sky thundered and the lightning played, but between storms the beating sun turned the woods tinder-dry; and when the lightning came again, Brandon began to fear a forest fire. But time was the real worry; time was relentless, always present and always gone. He pushed the crew, but he was no longer remote from his men; he had faced a fallacy that day at Boxed T and had since changed all his attitude. These men, too, had a stake in the race if you shared your need with them and thus made it theirs. A few restless ones, knowing Warlock to be near, slipped away to taste the pleasures of the boom camp; but most of the crew stuck, saving their thirst till deadline.

The days dwindled away until there were only a last couple left. No McCoy now, but still the shadow of Consolidated fell darkly. Let this Warlock contract be lost, and Consolidated would have another construction chief on the scene. That thought haunted Brandon and turned him desperate. With less than forty-eight hours to go, he called Jake Fargo to his tent after supper.

Fargo was getting touchy as a springtime bear. He had resisted Warlock's nearby saloons, and the strain of this resistance showed on him. He seated himself and gave Brandon a dour look and said, "We're beat, eh, Holt?"

Brandon hadn't shaved for five days. He supposed he looked as whiskery as Jake. He was silent for a moment, thinking of the hours lost when the crew had ridden to the hills after Gail, and the hours, another day, when they'd loitered at Boxed T, thinking of all the delays, little and big, and wishing he had those accumulated hours before him. A day now could make the difference.

Jake said sharply, "I said we're beat, Holt."

"Maybe not," Brandon said. "To fulfill the contract, we've got to have a wire into Warlock, one that will carry a message. That's all. From here on, we'll string to trees and only use poles where we can't bridge without them. If I have to suspend the wire from the shoulder of one man to another, I'll get it into Warlock. After we've sent a completion message, we can finish up proper."

Fargo merely stared. Then his whiskery face began to brighten, and he said, "It should bigawd work! You're right. The contract only calls for a workable wire."

Brandon said, "Tell the crew we're putting in another night shift."

They pushed on through that night and all the next day and into the next night. The wire was strung from branch to branch; the insulators were tacked to trees. Brandon worked feverishly, wishing this idea had come to him a few days earlier, wondering now if it had come too late. In the mountain meadows the crew set poles; and on the second night, outside Warlock, they came upon a length of sagging fence that had been put up when Warlock had known its first boom, years before. They strung the wire along this fence, and in the early morning came into Warlock, a scatteration of tents and shacks stuck between the weathered old log buildings of earlier days.

Warlock sat cramped on a shelf on the mountainside, and they brought the wire along the twisted street and set up their equipment in a deserted log cabin. The crew crowded into this little place. Brandon looked at the men around him and now let his hope soar.

"This should do it," he said.

Deadline today. Deadline, and the job nearly done. Brandon fumbled to open the line, having a last fear that somewhere a tree branch had failed to hold the wire and that it had fallen and broken. None of them had paused for breakfast this morning. He felt light-headed; he felt detached from all this yet infinitely concerned.

Fargo stood near him. Just a month and a day now since Jake had ridden back from his fruitless chase of McCoy and Lucas after that night attack on the camp, ridden back with a bullet-torn shoulder. Brandon said, "You send the completion message, Jake."

"Hell," Fargo said, startled, "you're the construction chief."

"And you're the man who's worked longest for Mountain Telegraph. Send it, Jake."

Fargo stepped up to the key. "Damn it, Holt, I'm rusty at this."

Brandon said, "You weren't so rusty the night you got drunk and ordered a payroll in my name."

Fargo grinned. "I figured maybe you were still sore at me for that, Holt."

He touched the key. He tapped out the message. He waited for his acknowledgment and got it. Sam Whitcomb was at the other end; Sam had got himself out of bed, doctor or no, for the message that might come this day. Brandon looked around at the crew. He expected them to cheer, but they didn't. Then he understood why, for he himself had only a feeling of deep satisfaction that the job was done; it wasn't a thing you could voice. Finally a man tried it. He said, "Well, we sure as hell built ourselves a telegraph line, Holt."

Brandon said, "That we did," and knew that he stood close to his men; this was a shared and abiding thing. He said, "Nothing more to do today, boys, but spend your pay. If there's a barber in camp, you'd better look him up. He could do a wholesale business with the bunch of you."

He shouldered his way among them and walked from the cabin and stood in the sunlight. Around him Warlock teemed; miners thronged the planking of this revived ghost town. Here, too, were the gamblers and the girls and all the other flotsam washed up on the crest of the boom. He walked along aimlessly at first. Remembering his own advice to his crew, he found a barber and got a haircut and a shave and paid the exorbitant price demanded for this service. Afterward he found a place to eat, and then he walked along the street again.

He felt empty in his idleness; he had been so long geared to the job that he was now lost. It was often thus when a race was run, but he could recall none that had been so close. He wanted something to do. True, there were poles to be set, but that work could come later, with no rush about it. He thought of Sam Whitcomb, unable to be up here and thus alone in his triumph save for the few Mountain Telegraph men who were in Salish. He knew that Sam would be expecting him to come and make a full report. He thought of Gail and the gift he hadn't been able to give her and knew that the time had come when he must at last face her. He got his piebald and sought out Jake Fargo.

He found the man before a plank-and-canvas saloon, so hastily erected that the lumber was still green and the canvas fresh. In an hour's time, Fargo had succeeded in getting himself four hours drunk. There was a telegraph man for you; he knew how to cut corners.

Fargo stood swaying before the saloon, a quart bottle in his hand. It was nearly empty, Brandon noticed.

Brandon said, "I'm riding to Salish, Jake. Tomorrow morning, get the boys to putting in those poles."

Fargo nodded solemnly. "Been looking for you, Holt. Been saving the heel of this bottle for you. A drink together?"

"Sure," Brandon said, and reached for the bottle.

"Me first," said Fargo. "Oldesh man with Mountain." He lifted the bottle. "Besides, got a toast to make." He squinted owlishly at Brandon. "Knew Creighton. Worked for him on Western Union. He was a telegraph man, Holt. Worked for another man back in the 'forties, when I was hardly dry behind the ears. Irishman named O'Rielly. Spelled his name different from all the rest of the O'Reillys. He strung wire in the Middle West and the South, that O'Rielly. Back in the days when a preacher could get his congregation to tear down a line by telling them the telegraph robbed the air of electricity. Claimed it hindered the rains and ruined the crops. 'S'fact, Holt. Ain't nobody ever heard of O'Rielly these days, but he built eight thousand miles of telegraph line. Patched his breaks with old stovepipes, if nothing else was handy. He was a bigawd telegraph man, Holt. The breed's dying out, but it ain't dead yet. I drink to O'Rielly, and to Creighton. And I drink to you, Holt."

He held the bottle up to the light, measuring the contents, and put his thumbnail at the halfway mark. He took a pull and made his inspection of what remained and handed the bottle to Brandon. Brandon finished it and tossed the empty away. Fargo looked at it forlornly, then brightened. "More where that come from." He again squinted at Brandon. "You've changed, Holt. Every man in camp has noticed it. It comes to my mind that I first marked the change that day we all rode to Boxed T. I was a scared man when we found McCoy had slipped his rope and got a horse and got away. Scared for you."

Brandon said, "It's done with now. Another range, another job."

Fargo said, "Damned if we don't get us a new bottle and drink to that!"

Brandon said, "Not today, Jake. I've got to ride."

He stopped at the cook's wagon long enough to pick up some food, and rode out of Warlock. He made his camp that night near the foot of the slope and saw the lights of Boxed T winking distantly. He rode through all the next day, not pushing himself, and the second night he slept near the rocks where Lucas had once besieged him. He hit Salish the following morning and heard the clang of a locomotive bell as he came into the street. This astonished him until he realized that time had meant progress for the railroad, too, and the steel had now come to Salish and thrust beyond the town. He'd followed the wagon road on the last miles and so had not been near the new rails.

At divisional headquarters, he made his inquiry and found that Whitcomb had moved from the Ballard House to his private car, which now stood on a siding here in Salish. He got a restaurant meal then and another barbershop shave. He walked along the street and found it strangely sedate; the wild and boisterous ones were gone, and he remembered faces at Warlock that had seemed familiar. That was the way of the boomers; they moved on, leaving their debris and an echo of their raucousness. The windows of the Hogshead were boarded; probably the owner was now running that plank-and-canvas place where Jake Fargo had drunk. Salish was again settling to a slow stride; someday, Brandon supposed, it would laud its wild past, just as a satisfied middle-aged man brags of his wicked youth. Maybe it would indeed be a town to be proud of in the future.

These reflections made him think of Doc King, and he looked about for King as he walked along. He found his man on the seat of a buckboard a block farther. King had pulled the buckboard up before a mercantile, and Ellen sat beside him. It was she who first spied Brandon and called his name.

He crossed over and pulled off his sombrero and said, "We finished the line."

Ellen said, "Yes, we heard." She was radiant; she was the loveliest thing in this day, and her radiance told him the truth before she spoke again. "Jonathan and I were married a week ago. We both wanted you present, but we knew you were racing toward your deadline."

King said, "I took your advice, Brandon." His gaiety was more than a veneer now; it was something that surged through him everlastingly and showed in his smile.

Brandon said, "I wish you both well." He looked to where a locomotive sent up black smoke. "I must be getting along."

Ellen said, "Come to Boxed T whenever you can, Holt. My father's up and about now."

"Sure," he said.

He walked on to where the new track lay. He was a thoughtful man, warmed by what he'd read in the faces of those two. He found the siding and Whitcomb's private car and set his fist to the door. Whitcomb let him in, brightening at the sight of him. Sam looked considerably thinner, but his face was no longer harassed. He silently escorted Brandon into the elegance of mahogany and red plush; and Whitcomb said then, "Sit down, son." Brandon did so. A heap softer than a saddle, this chair.

Whitcomb said, "You've turned in another fine piece of work, Holt. You already know what it means to the future of Mountain. If there's anything you want, name it."

Brandon shook his head. "There's nothing I want from you, Sam, that you haven't already given me."

Whitcomb nodded thoughtfully. "Yes, Gail told me," he said. "The whole story. Including how after the marriage you told her about Texas and why you felt bound to me. No true friendship can be based on one man's owing another, Holt. There'd be no good in it for either man. It would start being a matter of debits and credits with no true balance ever struck. I never counted you as bounden to me, son. It would have soured all the years I've known you."

"Yes," Brandon said, and he was remembering how he'd tried paying his debt to Boxed T in exact proportion, and what had nearly come of that. "I know it now. It was a thing that got crossways in my mind and stuck."

Whitcomb said, "The irony of it is that young Buck Elliot got pardoned years ago. By the President. I remember reading about it in the papers. I supposed that I'd told you at the time, but perhaps I was in Chicago and you were in the field. It's all so long ago and far away."

"Yes," Brandon said. "Dead and done with. But I'm glad for Buck."

He heard the door to the sleeping quarters open, and Gail stood there. She came toward him; she was wearing a calico dress today. He struggled to his feet. Her face showed Sam's new calmness and some of Sam's wisdom and understanding, but still this was for Brandon a bad moment. He had never known what he would say when the time came, and so the words were unbidden. "I just want to say this, Gail. First I gave Halliday a chance to leave town. That was to have been my present for you, but he didn't take it. In what happened next, I had no choice."

He heard another door open and shut, and this startled him. Sam had left the car. Brandon felt as though a prop had been taken away from him; he felt trapped and uncertain.

Gail said in a low voice, "Kirk was old enough to be interesting. He knew the words a girl wants to hear. My father has since pointed out that the rotten spot was always in him. That would have been a sad thing for me to have discovered after Missoula. Still, I don't wish him dead. It just seems to me, Holt, that he picked his own path." Her face began to break. "And it seems to me that I've been an utter fool."

Confederate bonds again. What frailty made each person sometime in his life pin his faith on a mistaken notion? He himself had done this for seventeen years in his own blind way. He said, "It doesn't need to matter, Gail. Unless you let it."

She shook her head. "It's not only that I picked the wrong man, but I was so willful about it. Dad had picked another man for me and told me so. So I got obstinate. If only he had let me find you for myself, it might have been different from the very first."

"Me?" He was truly astonished.

"Who else would my father have picked?"

This left him with nothing to say; he had only the sharp knowledge that for him she was the woman. He wondered when he'd first come to love her—in this car, or on the trail down from Hashknife's cabin, or in the wagon yard behind divisional headquarters when he'd stopped her and Halliday? He wondered, too, how the knowledge had been with him so long yet only now stood clear to him. He remembered the prairie flowers to which he'd been blind till they'd bloomed all around him. He felt awkward, and his hands seemed to be in his way. Finally he said, "I'm only sorry I had to use a gun at the wedding. For my part, I'd like the marriage to stand. But if you wish, it can be annulled."

"Yes," she said. "That's what the preacher's wife whispered to me, just as you suspected. But she also whispered something else. She said that any man who would risk force to make the girl marry him must want the girl mightily. She didn't understand that it was your loyalty to Sam Whitcomb that was moving you that day. But I've turned the whole thing over in my mind many times since. I think I would like to own a part of that loyalty, Holt. I think I would like to have it forever sheltering me no matter what wind might blow."

He said, "Then you mean—"

She looked up at him; she smiled. "I remember riding down the slope to Boxed T with Mountain's crew behind me. I remember seeing you on the porch with Ellen and knowing you were alive and safe. And I remember not wanting my face to show what I felt in that moment. A last willfulness, Holt; a last bit of feminine pride."

He shook his head, thinking of all the ranges across which the long lightning must yet be flung, thinking of the camps to come and the rough miles, but thinking, too, of the camp she had brightened. He said, "It isn't much of a life I can offer you."

She said, "I am Sam Whitcomb's daughter, so I shall not feel strange in a construction camp. You will find me much like him in many ways, Holt, sometimes to your sorrow." She moved closer to him. "There is no more I can tell you, no more I can offer."

Now she was within the reach of his hands, and he drew her to him. Her lips were warmer than they had been on their wedding day; he tasted her full response. He wondered what words to say, what pledge to make, but he remembered the wisdom of Sam Whitcomb that he himself had taken so long to learn. This must not be a bounden thing; this must hold no obligation but the heart's. He pressed her close and was a grateful man and a silent one; and after a long while he heard a door open, and he turned then to face Sam.

J.T. EDSON

Brings to Life the Fierce and Often Bloody Struggles of the Untamed West

THE BAD BUNCH	20764-9	$3.50
THE FASTEST GUN IN TEXAS	20818-1	$3.50
NO FINGER ON THE TRIGGER	20749-5	$3.50
SLIP GUN	20772-X	$3.50
TROUBLED RANGE	20773-8	$3.50
JUSTICE OF COMPANY Z	20858-0	$3.50
McGRAW'S INHERITANCE	20869-6	$3.50
RAPIDO CLINT	20868-8	$3.50
COMMANCHE	20930-7	$3.50
A MATTER OF HONOR	20936-6	$3.50
WACO RIDES IN	21019-4	$3.50
BLOODY BORDER	21031-3	$3.50
ALVIN FOG, TEXAS RANGER	21034-8	$3.50

FLOATING OUTFIT SERIES

THE HIDE AND TALLOW MEN	20862-9	$3.50
THE NIGHTHAWK	20726-6	$3.50
RENEGADE	20964-1	$3.50